"You must think I'm not much of a private investigator," Samantha said.

Will shook his head and smiled. "You're the most amazing woman I've ever met. You were just outnumbered. In a fair fight, I'd ⟨...⟩ on you any time, Sam."

He cupped h⟨...⟩ ⟨...⟩capable hand of a ⟨...⟩ She covered his ha⟨...⟩

"You sure you'll ⟨...⟩ here by yourself?" Will asked her, his blue eyes dark with obvious desire. "I could wash your back."

Samantha swallowed, consumed with the thought of the two of them in the tub. The temptation was almost too much.

From the doorway behind them came the sounds of the little boy in the next room.

"You better see to Zack."

He nodded and smiled. "Maybe another time," he whispered.

She'd underestimated this man, Samantha thought. Just as she'd underestimated how dangerous this case was. She wouldn't make either mistake again....

Dear Harlequin Intrigue Reader,

The recipe for a perfect Valentine's Day: chocolate, champagne—and four original romantic suspense titles from Harlequin Intrigue!

Our TOP SECRET BABIES promotion kicks off with Rita Herron's *Saving His Son* (#601). Devastated single mother Lindsey Payne suspects her child is alive and well—and being kept from her deliberately. The only man who'd be as determined as she is to find her child is Detective Gavin McCord—*if* he knew he'd fathered her missing baby....

In *Best-Kept Secrets* (#602) by Dani Sinclair, the tongues in MYSTERY JUNCTION are wagging about newcomer Jake Collins. Amy Thomas's first and only love has returned at last and she's ready to tell him the secret she's long kept hidden. But would revealing it suddenly put her life in jeopardy?

Our ON THE EDGE program continues with *Private Vows* (#603) by Sally Steward. A beautiful amnesiac is desperate to remember her past. Investigator Cole Grayson is desperate to keep it hidden. For if she remembers the truth, she'd never be his....

Bachelor Will Sheridan thinks he's found the perfect *Mystery Bride* (#604) in B.J. Daniels's latest romantic thriller. But the sexy and provocative Samantha Murphy is a female P.I. in the middle of a puzzling case when Will suddenly becomes her shadow. Now with desire distracting her and a child's life in the balance, Samantha and Will are about to discover the true meaning of "partnership"!

Next month more from TOP SECRET BABIES and ON THE EDGE, plus a 3-in-1 collection from some of your favorite authors and the launch of Sheryl Lynn's new McCLINTOCK COUNTRY miniseries.

Sincerely,

Denise O'Sullivan
Associate Senior Editor
Harlequin Intrigue

MYSTERY BRIDE
B.J. DANIELS

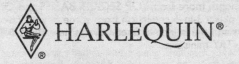

HARLEQUIN®

TORONTO • NEW YORK • LONDON
AMSTERDAM • PARIS • SYDNEY • HAMBURG
STOCKHOLM • ATHENS • TOKYO • MILAN • MADRID
PRAGUE • WARSAW • BUDAPEST • AUCKLAND

ISBN 0-373-22604-7

MYSTERY BRIDE

Copyright © 2001 by Barbara Heinlein.

This edition published by arrangement with Harlequin Books S.A.

® and TM are trademarks of the publisher. Trademarks indicated with ® are registered in the United States Patent and Trademark Office, the Canadian Trade Marks Office and in other countries.

Visit us at www.eHarlequin.com

Printed in U.S.A.

ABOUT THE AUTHOR

Born in Houston, B.J. Daniels is a former Southern girl who grew up on the smell of gulf sea air and Southern cooking. But like her characters, her home is now in Montana, not far from Big Sky, where she snowboards in the winters and boats in the summers with her husband and daughters. She does miss gumbo and Texas Barbecue, though! Her first Harlequin Intrigue novel was nominated for the *Romantic Times* Reviewer's Choice Award for best first book and best Harlequin Intrigue. She is a member of Romance Writers of America, Heart of Montana and Bozeman Writers group. B.J. loves to hear from readers. Write to her at P.O. Box 183, Bozeman, MT 59771.

Books by B.J. Daniels

HARLEQUIN INTRIGUE
312—ODD MAN OUT
353—OUTLAWED!
417—HOTSHOT P.I.
446—UNDERCOVER CHRISTMAS
493—A FATHER FOR HER BABY
533—STOLEN MOMENTS
555—LOVE AT FIRST SIGHT
566—INTIMATE SECRETS
585—THE AGENT'S SECRET CHILD
604—MYSTERY BRIDE

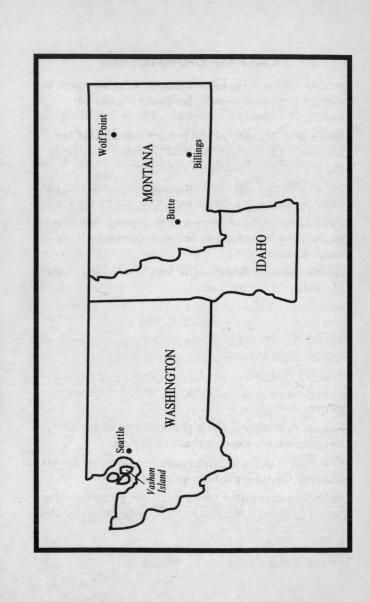

CAST OF CHARACTERS

Will Sheridan—He knows exactly what he wants in a bride. But some women, he discovers, can be murder.

Samantha Murphy—The private investigator has dreamed of a man just like Will Sheridan—but he is the last thing she needs on this case.

Lucas O'Brien—Is the computer game designer just being paranoid or is someone really out to get him?

Zack O'Brien—Everyone suddenly wants the five-year-old son of the game designer a little too desperately.

Cassie Clark O'Brien—The first ex-wife has a killer of a secret she must keep.

Mercedes Palmer O'Brien—The second ex-wife isn't one to carry a grudge. She gets even.

Al the Ox—The former wrestler turned kidnapper is just following orders. But whose orders?

Bradley Guess—Does the computer nerd really believe his partner has taken off with the missing game?

Robert A. Walker—He is philosophical about his investments. He expects them to pay off.

Eric Ross—Does he have reason to be afraid for his brother? Or is he playing a game of his own?

Bebe, the computer game designer groupie—She seems to know a lot about the missing game *and* the missing designer.

This one is for my first sister-in-law, Francis Demarais, of Malta, Montana, who taught me how to make bread and the best fudge in the world. You have been a constant in my life for many years now and one of its joys. Thanks for always keeping me a part of the family.

Prologue

Lucas heard the heavy tread of footsteps coming up the back stairs just as he finished burning the CD. In the dimly lit office, he popped the CD from the disk burner and grabbed one of the game boxes on his desk. Tossing the game's CD into the trash, he put his disk inside and snapped the box shut.

Hurriedly, he pried open the back of the computer and ripped out the memory board, smashing it on the floor with the sole of his shoe. Then he destroyed the CD burner and zip drive.

Just a few more minutes. He thought of his son waiting for him nearby at a friend's house and the train tickets he had bought for tonight. He heard a sound like a door closing somewhere in the office building.

He snapped off the desk lamp and moved to the fifth-floor window. On the street below, he spotted a figure hunkered in the shadows near the front door of the building.

He swore. Panicked, he picked up the stack of CDs

he'd burned. Five total. Five pieces of a puzzle he'd spent his life dreaming of solving. And finally had.

Another sound echoed up from the belly of the building.

They're coming. Destroy the CDs. Before it's too late.

But even as he thought it, he knew he couldn't. Not just because of all the years of work that had gone into them—but because of his son. Lucas needed to leave something behind. So far, he'd just left a trail of mistakes.

As he desperately looked around the office, he spotted the mail chute, and suddenly had an idea. Hurriedly, he scooped up the CDs and rushed into his outer office. Sitting down at the remaining intact computer, he typed out a note and made five copies of it.

He stopped to listen, but heard nothing beyond the usual creaking and groaning of the old building. But he knew he was no longer alone.

As quickly as he could, he addressed five envelopes, stamped them and began slipping the note and a CD into each.

Just as he was about to put the last CD into the envelope addressed to one Samantha Murphy of Butte, Montana, he heard footfalls. The stairway door down the hall groaned open.

But what stopped him dead was the sound of small feet running down the worn carpeting toward his office and a single cried word. "Daddy!"

Oh, God. Zack.

He dropped the final CD to the floor, his heart catching in his throat, as his five-year-old son came running into his office. With dark eyes wild with fear, Zack threw himself into his father's arms.

"Daddy, they made me get in the car. I didn't want to. But I kicked the big guy and got away and ran—"

"It's okay, Zack," he said, hugging his son. He could hear the sound of footsteps coming down the hall, slow and steady. They knew they had him trapped. They just didn't realize how desperate he was.

With Zack still in his arms, he ripped out the mother board from the last remaining computer in his office, destroyed it, then rushed to lock the outer office door. Then grabbing up the envelopes and the fallen CD, he hurried them into his office and locked the door, knowing it was only a stopgap measure. There was no escape now.

He put Zack down and knelt beside him. Zack wore the little red jacket Lucas had bought him for the flight and the navy backpack they'd loaded with a few of his favorite toys. After all, they'd be traveling light.

"Are you all right?" he asked his son.

Zack nodded and put on his little tough-guy face.

It was all Lucas could do not to break down at the sight. He struggled, with his emotions, with his frantic thoughts. The men after him had known where to find Zack. This changed things, Lucas realized.

His mind scrambled for an out. But he knew there wasn't one. Trying to hide the CDs would be futile. Destroying them wouldn't save his son. Just the opposite.

Something heavy slammed against the outer office door, rattling the windows. Resigned, he did the only thing he could. He picked up the four CDs already in the addressed envelopes and dropped them down the mail chute. The sound of them sliding down to the first floor mail drop was muffled by the splintering of wood at his outer office door.

Lucas picked up the fifth CD box, and praying he was doing the right thing, slipped it into his son's backpack, then he opened his desk drawer and started to take out the loaded .38. Earlier he'd been prepared to kill anyone who tried to stop him. Now, he glanced at his son and slowly closed the desk drawer without removing the gun.

Everything had changed.

He picked Zack up again and hugged him fiercely, committing to memory the feel of his son in his arms, fearing he'd never hold him again. His son. Of all his regrets, Zack was at the top of the list.

"Listen to me, Zack," he said as the outer office door gave way with a loud crash. "I need you to be strong and very brave."

Zack looked up at him, his eyes fearful, but full of trust and love.

Lucas explained what the boy had to do.

Zack nodded, tears in his eyes. "I will be very brave," he said, his small body trembling.

Something large and heavy hit his office door with a resounding boom.

He lowered his son down on the floor. "Get under the desk and remember what I said." The boy scrambled back into the hole. "Zack? I'm sorry about all this. I love you."

Chapter One

Billings, Montana
Friday night

Samantha Murphy slipped off her high heels, shimmied her dress up to her hips and began to climb the rock wall. As she dropped to the patio on the other side, she heard the sound of fabric tearing. No more silk for undercover work.

She tugged down her dress, inspecting the rip up the right side clear to her knee. *Great,* she thought, as she slid back into her heels. Belatedly she realized she wasn't alone.

"Champagne, miss?"

She spun around to find a waiter holding a tray filled with sparkling glasses. Behind him through the closed French doors to the house, she could hear the faint sound of classical music, the gentle tinkle of glasses and soft murmured conversation.

She and the waiter were alone on the patio, no doubt each wondering what the other was doing there. She had the distinct impression that he'd probably been taking a breather from the party and had caught her "revealing" grand entrance. She was glad she hadn't worn her thong underwear.

While his expression remained impassive, she could have sworn she caught a glint of amusement in his eyes as he held out the tray.

Her cheeks warmed as she took a glass. "Thank you, I *could* use a drink."

He gave her a slight nod and then moved to the French doors, opening them wide before disappearing inside.

She took a sip of the bubbly and watched him. While she doubted he'd go to the trouble of telling the hostess that a party crasher had just landed on the patio, she had every reason to be anxious. Through the open doors she could see men in tuxedos and women in expensive, formal gowns standing around making idle conversation over canapés and cocktails. She couldn't have felt more out of place at a nudist colony.

She took another sip of the champagne and headed for the French doors.

But just before she reached them, she caught her reflection in the polished glass. She hardly recognized herself. The white silk dress hugged her curves—the rip up the right side seam almost looked as if the dress had come that way; the strappy high heels added a much-desired three inches to her slight five-foot-four frame; the sophisticated hairdo swept her usually wild mane up into an intricate maze of perky curls and strategically located tendrils that framed her perfectly made-up face.

"Not bad," she whispered. Her own mother wouldn't recognize her.

Feeling like Cinderella at the ball, she gave the

woman in the glass a conspiratorial wink, checked to make sure the miniature camera was still snug in her bra between her breasts, and then braced herself. Chin up. Stomach in. *Show time.*

Will Sheridan knew what he was looking for. He stood at the edge of the party, searching the crowd. He'd planned this, just as he'd planned everything else in his life. Now with his thirty-sixth birthday approaching, he was ready for the next step. Marriage.

That decision made, it was just a matter of finding his perfect mate before his birthday—his self-imposed deadline. He wasn't worried. He'd taken some time off from his business to get the situation settled. He approached it as he had everything else in his life: methodically. Find the woman, romance her and, after the proper amount of time, marry her.

And he knew *exactly* what he wanted in a wife, so he didn't think it would be difficult. It was one of the reasons he'd accepted his sister's invitation. Katherine Sheridan Ashley threw the kind of parties he assumed his prospective wife would attend. The woman of his dreams would no doubt travel in these circles, have a career that complemented his, share a similar family background with these people, and have the refined tastes that would make her the perfect wife and mother of his children.

Used to consulting experts when he needed advanced expertise, he'd agreed to attend one of his sister's many parties at her grand home on the rimrocks overlooking Billings. It was as high society as he could take.

Katherine had assured him he wouldn't be disappointed. She had just the woman in mind for him.

Not that he thought he'd need much help. In fact, he firmly believed that he'd know his future wife the moment he saw her. That's why he wasn't the least bit surprised when she appeared like a vision, stepping in from the night through the ornate French patio doors in a white gown.

SAMANTHA WORKED HER WAY through the party crowd, smiling, nodding, exchanging pleasantries, looking for a man. She knew exactly what she was looking for and wasn't surprised when—after a couple of canapés and another glass of champagne, consumed only as part of her cover, of course—she found him.

Stealthily, she studied the man from a distance, recognizing him from the black-and-white photograph she'd been given. A second man approached him, and the two took their conversation down the hallway to a far wing of the rambling dwelling.

With the floor plan fresh in her memory, she eased out a side door away from the crowd. Slipping off her heels again and holding them in one hand she hoisted her dress and raced around the perimeter via the many patios, until she found herself directly outside the library. She put her heels back on, then standing breathlessly in the dark, she watched from behind a large, leafy plant as the first man withdrew a wad of bills from his tuxedo jacket. He handed them to the second man in exchange for a manila envelope.

From her bra, she pulled out the camera and snapped a couple of quick shots as the two men made the exchange. As the first man took the envelope over to the desk, turned on the desk lamp and pulled out the contents, the second man counted the money.

She zoomed in and took another shot of what were clearly bids for the new highway construction project. As she moved to get one final incriminating photo, she bumped into the huge flowerpot with a resounding *thunk*.

The men in the library looked up—right in her direction, although she knew they couldn't see her. Yet. The first man drew a gun as he moved toward the patio—and her.

"Hello."

She jumped at the sound of a male voice directly behind her. Hurriedly sliding the camera back into her bra and praying everything was safely covered inside her snug-fitting dress, she swung around, ready to defend herself if necessary.

She'd half expected the man behind her to be the waiter she'd met earlier, although she feared if it was, he wouldn't be offering her champagne this time.

It wasn't the waiter. Far from it.

This man was tall, broad-shouldered, and dressed in a tuxedo. She had to look up to see his face, and although only faint light leaked from the library window, she caught her breath at the sight of him. Not a woman to be knocked off her high heels by simple good looks, she felt herself wobble just a little. He had a strong masculine jaw, classic features and thick dark hair. A pair of intense blue eyes the color of faded denim peered at her through small wire-rimmed glasses. He was so close she could smell his faint aftershave. Umm.

He held two full champagne glasses and smiled

tentatively at her. His smile set the air around her vibrating. Goose bumps rose on her skin, and she swore the hair on the back of her neck stood on end—not to mention what he was doing to the rest of her.

"Hello," he said again. His voice was deep and soft. Hypnotic. His denim-eyed gaze was intent.

For just an instant, she lost herself in all that heavenly blue. Then the sound of footsteps behind her in the library jerked her back to earth. Any moment, she knew the library door would burst open and the men she'd photographed would see her. And get the wrong impression. Actually, the right impression, in this case. An impression that could get her and this handsome stranger killed.

She always had a backup plan. Sans a plan, she punted.

Impulsively, she threw her arms around the man's neck and kissed him. He stiffened in surprise. But there wasn't much he could do, considering both his hands held champagne glasses. She heard the library door bang open as she buried her fingers in the stranger's thick, lush hair and deepened the kiss, listening behind her for the familiar sound of a bolt sliding back on a weapon just before it was fired.

To his credit, it took him only seconds. He tossed the champagne glasses over his shoulder and pulled her into his arms, kissing her back with nothing short of wanton abandon. She barely even heard the champagne glasses break on the rock wall behind them as he stole more than her breath.

She surfaced slowly from the kiss, letting out a small satisfied sigh as he leisurely lifted his lips from hers. She blinked, then glanced around in confusion.

The patio was empty except for the two of them; the library door was closed, the lights extinguished, the two men gone. She hadn't even heard them leave. She hadn't heard anything but her pulse roaring in her ears and the erratic *thump* of her heart.

She looked up at the stranger in whose arms she was still enveloped.

He looked as stunned as she felt. "Wow," he said as he pulled back, his expression clearly shocked and…a little uncertain? "So much for idle chitchat."

She felt her face flush. "I—"

"Please, don't apologize. I'm flattered." He offered her his hand. "I don't believe we've been formally introduced. I'm Will Sheridan."

His large, warm hand closed over hers.

"Sam-Samantha—" she stammered. "Moore." Or less. "Samantha Moore."

He smiled again, and she felt his powerful force field pulling her in.

"I'm delighted to finally meet you," he said in that soft, deep voice of his. "I can't tell you how long I've waited for this." He sounded a little embarrassed. "Although, I have to admit, it didn't go quite like I'd planned it."

Was he saying he knew her? She was sure she'd never met him before. He wasn't the kind of man she'd forget. One thing she was sure of: she'd never kissed him before. But she definitely wouldn't mind kissing him again.

"You took me by surprise," she stammered. Especially his kiss. Boy howdy.

"Trust me, not half as much as you did me."

His laugh warmed her like summer sunshine.

"You have a great smile. I want to know everything about you."

She doubted that. Still, she felt her cheeks redden from the heat of his gaze. This man could charm a woman right out of her high heels.

"Could we go somewhere and get better acquainted?" he asked excitedly. "I really do want to know *everything* about you."

That was the problem with kissing a man the first time you laid eyes on him. He often got the wrong idea. But she *did* want to get out of here, and the quicker the better.

She was just fumbling for an excuse to escape when her eye caught a movement. A woman appeared behind him. The smell of perfume reached her before the woman did.

"Will?" the woman enquired.

As he turned at the sound, Samantha quickly stepped back into the shadows.

"Will! What are you doing out here?"

The woman was dressed to kill and was obviously their hostess, Katherine Ashley. If her pinched tone and the frown on her face were any indication, she wasn't happy to see Will out here in the dark.

Samantha had a feeling Katherine Ashley would be even less happy to find him out here in the dark with an uninvited guest, especially one who was here to bust two of her *invited* guests. Seeing her chance, Samantha edged along the doorway in the dark and ducked behind the potted plant she'd bumped into earlier. Quietly she slipped into the unlit library.

"I've been looking all over for you, Will," she heard Katherine Ashley say. "I want you to meet the woman I told you about."

"I've already met—"

Samantha glanced back from the darkness of the library and saw him turn to introduce her. She felt a tug of regret as she saw his surprise to find her gone. Surprise—and disappointment?

She grimaced as she was smacked with a good strong jolt of guilt. Will Sheridan had come along just when she'd needed him. She hated to think what might have happened if she'd been caught alone outside the library by the men she'd photographed. He'd saved her bacon. Not to mention the added bonus of his kiss. Under other circumstances—

She put the thought out of her head. Although it had never come up before, she never got romantically involved while on a case.

She made her way back to the rock wall where she'd started, and, checking to make sure the coast was clear, slipped off her heels, wriggled up her dress and shimmied over the stones again. As she dropped to the expanse of manicured lawn that stretched between her and the road where her Mustang convertible was hidden in a clump of trees, she heard the silk rip again. This time all the way to her thigh.

Holding the dress up around her hips and her heels, she jogged barefoot through the darkness to the car. Once behind the wheel, she tossed her heels into the back seat and picked up her cell phone.

"I've got the photos," she said the moment the line was answered. "You're info was right about the commissioner. He *is* selling construction bids."

"Good work. That didn't take long. I assume it was uneventful?"

Absently she ran her tongue over her lips. "You know how these parties are."

''Send me the film, and I'll take it from here.''

She hung up, suddenly anxious to get moving. The ball was over. It was time for Cinderella to get home.

Too bad she hadn't left the prince a glass slipper so he could find her again. Instead, she'd given him a false name and disappeared on him. Some princess she was.

Well, if she ever saw him again— Like there was any chance of that. She didn't even live in the same city, and definitely didn't travel in the same circles.

''So long, Will Sheridan,'' she whispered as she pulled away and glanced in her rearview mirror. The road behind her was empty. What had she expected, Will to come after her?

Shaking her head at her own foolishness, she picked up the phone again and checked her messages. With a little luck, she might be able to sleep in tomorrow, since she had a long drive ahead of her tonight.

''Sam—?''

Her heart began to pound at the once oh-so-familiar voice on her machine.

''It's Lucas.''

As if he had to tell her. On key, her heart began to ache. Funny, but even after all these years just the sound of him could still make her hurt. *Lucas.* She swore under her breath and almost missed the rest of his message.

''I need your help, Sam. I'm in trouble. I need you to look after—''

She heard a noise in the background. Then silence.

She stared at the phone in disbelief. She hadn't even realized he knew where to find her. And now, after all these years and everything that had happened, Lucas had the nerve to call her out of the blue and say, *"Hey, I'm in trouble. I need your help. Look after—"* After what? His dog? His cat? His boat? His finances? Her heart began to beat harder. Oh God, surely he wasn't going to say his son? Zack? But why call her? Why not call Zack's mother?

She dialed Seattle information, got Lucas's home number and called it. The line rang and rang.

She hung up, unable to shake the scared feeling that had settled around her heart. Distracted, she barely noticed the dark-colored van that pulled out after her a few blocks from the party.

Normally, she could lose herself behind the wheel. Especially in the convertible with the top down. But on the five-hour drive home to Butte, not even speed, the cool fall night or letting her hair down could keep her from thinking about the party, Will Sheridan, the kiss and Lucas's call.

When she pulled into her driveway a little after 2:00 a.m., she saw in the headlights that something was terribly wrong. The front door of her small house stood open. She pulled her .357 from beneath the seat and carefully opened the car door.

The night was black, the shadows hunkering in the bushes around the house even blacker. A deathly quiet hung over the neighborhood. Not even the dog down the street barked.

As she padded barefoot to the front door, she raised the weapon, bracing herself for whatever might be waiting inside. The place had been ransacked. She wasn't overly neat, but she could see the damage the moment she stepped in. A faint light leaked out of the kitchen, spilling across the cluttered floor.

She swore under her breath. Why would someone do this? It wasn't as if she had much of value to steal. Behind her, through the still-open doorway, she heard a car engine. She turned in time to see a dark-colored van cruise by. It was too dark to see the driver, not that she paid that much attention. The van continued on down the street, the sound of its engine dying away as she turned back to her vandalized house.

She quickly searched the two floors. Nothing seemed to be missing, not that she could really tell in all this mess. The thing was, whoever had broken in hadn't bothered with her TV, stereo, VCR or the two good paintings she'd purchased for the living room. That about covered everything of value.

Once sure the burglar was not inside, she locked up and dialed 911, requesting her father, knowing she was in for a lecture on security systems.

She had barely hung up from talking with him when the phone rang, making her jump. Trying to still her racing pulse, she picked up the receiver, expecting to hear Lucas's voice.

"Samantha?"

Talk about *déjà vu.* Another blast from the past. Memories drifted over her like confetti—bright-colored vivid flashes of the past. Almost all of it painful.

"Cassie?"

It had been years since she'd heard from her former college roommate. Not since Cassie's wedding to Lucas. Certainly not since Cassie's divorce from Lucas a year later.

In those few seconds, she wondered what Cassie had been doing the past five years. It beat wondering what would've happened if Lucas had never met Cassie.

"I know it's been a long time—" Cassie sounded apologetic.

The call shouldn't have come as a surprise. Not after the one from Lucas.

But there was something else in Cassie's tone that made her wary. "What's wrong?" she asked, remembering Lucas's cryptic message on her machine.

"Have you heard from Lucas?" Cassie asked.

Her heart began to pound again. "Just a short message on my machine. I tried to call him, but I didn't get an answer."

"Have you talked to him lately?" Cassie asked, sounding hesitant.

"No." She hated to admit that she hadn't even thought of Lucas in a long time. The great love of her life. The great loss of her life. When had she quit thinking about him every minute of every day?

"Or received a letter or maybe a package from him?" Cassie asked, her voice taut.

Heart racing, Sam asked, "Cassie, what's happened?"

"Lucas has disappeared and Zack—" Cassie's voice broke. "Oh, Sam, I need your help."

Chapter Two

Wolf Point, Montana
Two days later

Will Sheridan prided himself on his tenacity. Samantha's sudden disappearance the night of the party had left him all the more eager to find her.

But before very long he'd realized it wasn't going to be as simple as he'd hoped. There was no Samantha Moore listed in the phone book. Nor did any of the Moores listed in Billings, Montana, know of a Samantha who fit her description.

Worse, when he'd called his sister, she'd been distracted over the commissioner's recent resignation.

"He's being investigated for corruption—corruption, mind you. And he was at *my* party," she cried. "Can you imagine? A criminal at one of my parties?"

"Alleged criminal," he noted distractedly, then quickly asked her about Samantha Moore.

Katherine assured him that no one by the name of Samantha Moore had been invited to the party—not as a guest or as a date of an invited guest.

"Are you sure you didn't just imagine this woman?"

His sister had sounded a little peeved because he hadn't cared for the woman she'd had in mind for him. Not that Jennifer Finley hadn't been adequate.

But she was no Samantha Moore. After Samantha, no other woman held any interest for him.

There were, however, several things about her that did cause him concern. The first of which was the Sudden and Sensuous Kiss.

And the fact that she'd literally disappeared from the party afterward. Why was that? He might have thought her shy, if not for the kiss. Or perhaps she hadn't wanted Katherine to see her, since Samantha wasn't, it appeared, an invited guest. Another small concern.

Neither explanation seemed to fit, but whatever the reason for her disappearance, he intended to find her. And he'd told Katherine as much.

"I just hope you know what you're getting into," she'd said haughtily before hanging up.

Did he? He'd assured himself with his usual confidence that he could handle whatever there was to learn about the woman. After all, unless he was completely wrong about her, she was going to be his wife.

And he was seldom wrong about things.

Two days later, on a hot, late-fall afternoon, he found her quite by accident. She was sitting in a blue Firebird in Wolf Point, Montana, her attention on something in the opposite direction from him.

He'd literally done a double take when he saw her as he drove past. She didn't look anything like she had at Katherine's party. And yet, he'd have known her anywhere.

His first impulse was to get out of his car and walk up to her driver's window. She had it rolled down, and was leaning back in the seat as if waiting for someone in the shade of the trees lining the quiet street.

He pulled over half a block past her car and walked back, coming up behind the Firebird. The car had plates for Silverbow County—a county clear across the state from where he'd first seen her. He wondered what she was doing in Wolf Point—sitting in a car this far from home. If her home even *was* in Silverbow County. And the car seemed all wrong for the woman he'd met at the party. Maybe she'd borrowed it from a friend.

As he approached the Firebird on the passenger side, watching the side mirror as he advanced, he was even more intrigued by this woman. Strangely, he had the feeling she might bolt if she saw him. Or maybe not so strangely. After all, she *had* disappeared from the party without a word—*and* after that very intimate kiss.

He'd almost reached her car when he heard the engine turn over. He wasn't about to let her get away again. Impulsively, he rushed forward, grabbed the passenger side door handle and pulled. The door swung open, and he jumped in.

SURPRISE DIDN'T EVEN come close to describing what Samantha felt when Will Sheridan leapt into the front seat of the Firebird. Her hand went for the pistol duct-taped beneath her seat—stopping just short of the weapon when she recognized him.

"Hello," he said, reminiscent of their first encounter. Except for the lack of champagne.

"Will Sheridan?" She stared at him openmouthed and tried to get her heart rate back to near normal.

He grinned. "You remembered."

Not likely that she'd forget. However, she'd never dreamed she'd see him again. And certainly not here. Certainly not now. What could the man possibly be doing so far from where she'd met him? Not to mention his timing, which was nothing short of amazingly bad.

"What are you doing here?" she demanded.

"Looking for you."

Oh, no, this didn't sound good. He must have found out that she was the one who busted the commissioner at his sister's party.

"Imagine running into you here in Wolf Point," he said, his look questioning, suspicious. Not surprising under the circumstances.

It was beyond even *her* imagination. She'd sized up Will Sheridan at the party and had known, even before she investigated him later, what kind of man he was. A stable, successful construction company owner with good standing in the community. Everything a woman could want. *If* that woman liked predictable and unimaginative. And terrible timing.

"Why were you looking for me?" she asked, already knowing the answer, wondering how she could get rid of him—short of shooting him.

"We didn't get to talk the other night at the party."

That stopped her. "What?"

He grinned. "I want to get to know you."

She stared at him. He had to be kidding. "Why?"

It was the kiss, dummy.

Pleeeeze. I'll admit it *was* a nice kiss—

Oh, come on. Can you even remember the last time a man made you feel like that?

Let's not even go *there.*

"Why?" He laughed. "I should think it's obvious."

It *was* the kiss. She dragged her gaze away to look down the street at the tan rental car parked in front of the motel. Time was running out. She had to do something. And quick.

She tried to keep the urgency out of her voice. "Will, I'm flattered but this really isn't a good time." Major understatement.

He seemed to notice then how she was dressed. A jogging bra that showed a lot of cleavage and midriff. A pair of skimpy running shorts. Cross-trainers and ankle socks. No makeup. Her unruly sun-streaked brown hair was pulled back in a ponytail. She was amazed he'd even recognized her.

"I guess my timing isn't very good?"

Boy howdy.

He smiled and reached for the door handle. She never knew she could feel relief *and* disappointment at the same time.

But he didn't get out.

"Here's the thing. I had a little bit of a hard time finding you," he said, turning back to her. He flashed her a hundred-watt smile. "Now, I'm afraid if I let you out of my sight you'll disappear again, and I might not be so lucky next time."

She stared at him. How *had* he found her? That was some luck.

Could be fate.

Yeah, right.

''So,'' he said, appearing as conflicted as she felt.

She could understand his confusion. She'd kissed him at first sight, lied to him and disappeared. Now here she was in this rather revealing outfit in a different town, acting even more strangely. Add to that the fact that he must have gone to a lot of trouble looking for her. By now he'd know she'd lied about her name and a lot more. And here she was trying desperately to get rid of him. What he must think!

So why was he still here? Why didn't he just turn and run?

THE LAST THING on Will Sheridan's mind was running. Admittedly, the situation was odd, and it appeared things wouldn't be quite as easy as he first might have hoped. But that had never stopped him when he wanted something.

And he wanted Samantha. When he looked at her he was struck by one clear thought: he wouldn't mind waking up to that face every morning. Tiny freckles trailed across the bridge of a cute little nose, golden lashes framed wide warm sea-green eyes, suntanned skin glowed on prominent cheekbones.

She'd been stunning at the party. But without makeup, she looked…delectable.

It wasn't just her face or her lovely body—something he could see a lot of right now. There was something…intriguing about this woman. Mysterious.

''So,'' he said again, hoping she'd help him out. He watched her shoot a glance down the block in the same direction she'd been looking when he'd first seen her. He followed her gaze down the quiet street to what appeared to be a small, one-story nursing home. The sign in front read, Lazy Rest. A tan Buick was parked in the for-the-disabled space out front. The car had a rental sticker on it but no disabled decal.

He could feel her tension. It was as strong as the low-frequency hum that vibrated between them. Was she meeting someone? Was that why she wanted him out of the car? She wasn't wearing a wedding ring, but that didn't mean she wasn't involved. Temporarily, he hoped.

"If I could just get your phone number," he said, wanting so much more. Home address, work number, e-mail, social security number and first-grade school photo. "I'd like to call you for a date, to start with—"

Her gaze swung around to his, her eyes wide. "You tracked me down just to ask me for a date—?"

She sounded incredulous. And almost suspicious. As if there was some other reason she thought he'd come looking for her.

"—To *start* with?"

Definitely suspicious now. Imagine what she'd say if he told her his real intention.

Up the block, the front doors of the rest home opened and a short, stocky man in his late thirties came down the long walkway. Was this the man she'd been waiting for? Shorty headed for the tan Buick parked at the curb.

Samantha seemed to catch the movement out of the corner of her eye. She swung around in her seat to stare in the man's direction, tense as a tightrope walker.

"Look, you seem busy. What are you doing to-night?"

"Tonight wouldn't be good," she said, her gaze on the man now opening the driver's door of the Buick. "Why don't I call you?"

Did she really think she could get rid of him that easily? "Samantha, I have no idea what's going on here, but I'm not getting out of this car until you at least talk to me. If you hadn't kissed me the way you had—"

SO IT *HAD* BEEN that blamed kiss! She'd regretted it for two days now. But only because she hadn't been able to put it—or Will Sheridan—out of her mind. She'd wondered, what if... What if they'd met under different circumstances. What if she ran into him again?

And now she had. And at the worst possible time!

She glanced over at him. One look, and she knew he meant what he'd said. He *wasn't* getting out of her car until he got some answers. Not that she could blame him. But he was making this very difficult.

She looked back to see the man getting into the rental car look back toward the nursing home, and she knew what she was going to have to do.

This is just part of the job.

Sure it is.

She threw herself into Will's arms and kissed him. Again. Only this time she didn't lose herself in his kiss. This time she kept it short and sweet. She couldn't afford not to.

WILL DREW BACK from the kiss, startled by the distinct *click* that reverberated through the Firebird. He felt something cold and metallic, looked down at his right wrist, and was shocked to see the handcuff there. Instinctively, he pulled, only to find the other end attached to a piece of steel that had been welded under the dash. How convenient.

"Samantha?" he asked, feeling a little disoriented.

"Will, I hate to do this, but you left me no choice." She slid out of the car before he could ask exactly what she hated to do. "Stay here. I'll be back."

Like he was going anywhere. "Samantha?" But she was already gone, jogging toward the Lazy Rest. He thought about calling after her as he watched her run, her ponytail pendulumming back and forth—but he didn't. What would be the point? He doubted she'd have handcuffed him to the car if anything had been up for discussion.

The short guy who'd come out of the rest home was standing by the car, looking around. He seemed edgy when he saw Samantha. Will couldn't blame him.

She'd almost reached the tan Buick and Shorty, when she stopped beneath a large willow tree and leaned with her palms against the thick trunk to stretch her calves. Very nice calves, he noticed.

The man beside the Buick, he saw, was noticing, as well.

Just then, another man came out of the rest home, this one taller and a little less stocky, but definitely muscular. He had a kid with him, a small boy wearing a Mariners baseball cap and a navy backpack over his red jacket. The kid had the cap pulled down so low his ears stood out like thumbs from his head;

a pair of headphones hung around his neck; and he cradled what looked like a CD player in his hands.

The man had one hand on the boy's shoulder. He looked around, and noticed Samantha stretching.

Samantha straightened and started jogging again— right toward them. The man's steps slowed as he and the boy approached the Buick, and Shorty, who was waiting there.

Samantha didn't appear to notice as she jogged in their direction, but Will had the distinct impression she was watching them. That she'd been waiting for them to come out. And if she kept running she'd connect with them in a matter of—

"What the—"

To his amazement, Samantha tripped and fell. She tumbled onto the lawn just feet from them and grabbed at her ankle. From where he sat, he heard her cry out in pain.

He jerked on the handcuff, wanting to go to her. What had the woman been thinking, locking him up like this?

The two men seemed startled, almost leery of her, and glanced around as if looking for something or someone. The quiet neighborhood dozed in the warm fall afternoon sun as Samantha cried and hugged her ankle.

After a moment, they hesitantly stepped over to her. No doubt her skimpy attire helped convince them.

Will couldn't hear what was being said even though the driver's window of the Firebird was still down, but it was obvious they were offering some sort of assistance. The short one helped her to her feet. The second man released the boy to take her other arm.

She appeared afraid to put weight on her injured ankle. Slowly, she attempted a step.

Then everything happened so fast Will wasn't even sure later what he'd seen. Maybe because he was hoping he'd just imagined it.

He watched in horror as Samantha dropped Shorty with a swift kick, sent the other man sprawling face-first onto the grass with some sort of karate chop, and grabbed the kid.

In the blink of an eye, Samantha was running back toward the Firebird with the boy in her arms. She opened the driver's door, tossed him the kid and leaped in.

The Firebird engine roared, and she peeled out, throwing gravel and dust as she whipped a cookie in the middle of the street, then took off in a tremulous thunder of engine and speed that flattened him against his seat.

"Wow," the kid said.

"Samantha?" Will asked quietly, the way he might talk to a disturbed patient on a mental ward. "I know this probably isn't a good time, either, but could you tell me what's going on here?"

The Firebird screamed around a corner. "I'd suggest you get the boy buckled in," she said calmly. "You might want to do the same."

Being handcuffed to the dash didn't make the task easy, but as she took the next corner on two wheels, Will managed to get the kid buckled in between them on the bench seat before the Firebird rocked back down on all four tires. He snapped his own seat belt as she took a gravel-throwing turn.

"Nice car," the kid said.

Will looked down at him. The boy was all of five, with large brown eyes that twinkled in a positively angelic face. Along with the Mariners cap and red jacket, he wore faded worn jeans, a Pokémon T-shirt and sneakers. The headphones still hung around his neck, with a cord that ran to the CD player cradled in his lap on the small navy backpack. Unlike Will, the boy didn't seem all that surprised by this turn of events.

Will turned to catch sight of the Buick coming up fast. *Great.* "Just tell me you don't kidnap children. I mean, this isn't just some random thing you do, right? You know this child, right?" He looked expectantly at her, waiting.

"Only from a faxed photo of him. He's cuter in person." She shot the kid a quick smile, then went back to her driving, which Will was thankful for. "His name is Zackarias Lucien O'Brien, age five-and-a-half, of Seattle, Washington. That about covers it."

"Just 'Zack,'" the boy said quickly. "Just Zack" didn't appear in the least upset as Sam took a turn on two wheels.

"Am I missing something here?" Will asked.

Samantha turned onto a paved two-lane and tromped down on the gas. The car took off like a rocket.

"What is under the hood?" he yelled over the roar of the engine.

She shot him a grin. "You like it?"

Not really. He liked it when he thought she was someone else: a nice, single woman who drove a Lexus.

''Sorry about the cuffs, but I couldn't let you ruin my show.''

She made the whole thing sound theatrical and almost innocent. He nodded, telling himself again that she'd have a good explanation for this. It was just getting harder to believe.

She glanced over her shoulder. He looked back, too. The Buick wasn't far behind them now.

''And those men?'' he enquired.

She shrugged. ''Your guess is as good as mine.'' She looked over at Zack. ''Who are those guys?''

He shrugged, too. ''They said they were friends of my birth mother's.''

She raised a brow as she looked at the boy.

Will wished she'd keep her eyes on the road. Not that she didn't seem capable of doing any number of things while driving. ''Where exactly are we headed?'' he asked, as the flat landscape flashed by in a blur and he realized they'd left Wolf Point far behind.

''Seattle, eventually. Right now—'' she glanced into her rearview mirror ''—anyplace where *they* aren't,'' she said, indicating the Buick gaining on them.

Seattle? He thought about telling her that Seattle didn't fit into his plans. But what she did next made him lose the thought.

He watched her reach under the seat, pull out a handgun and lay it across her sun-browned thighs. He told himself he shouldn't have been surprised, but he was. How could he have been so wrong about a woman?

He wondered what Jennifer Finley was doing right now.

"You can just drop me off when you get the chance," he said—not that she seemed to be listening. "Anywhere would do." He noted that the Firebird was pegged at over a hundred miles an hour and that the Buick was right behind them.

"See that box on the floor at your feet?" she asked.

He looked down to see a cardboard box about eight inches square. "Yes?"

"I'd appreciate it if you'd pick it up."

Amazingly, it didn't seem like such a strange request, all things considered.

He rattled the handcuff. "I'm not sure I can do it locked to your dash."

She shot a look at him. "Oh, I think you can handle it."

He wasn't sure that was a compliment. Worse, it appeared she wasn't ready to uncuff him.

He lifted the box from the floor with his free hand. It was much heavier than he'd expected. "What's in here—iron?"

She didn't answer.

He turned back the cardboard flaps on the box. At first it looked like a box full of children's jacks, the kind his sister used to play with. Only these jacks were huge. But as he looked closer he saw that the box was packed with sixteen-penny nails welded together and ends sharpened to make large, ugly-looking multi-sided spikes.

He looked at her askance. He was in the construction business but had no idea where anyone would buy something like this, or let alone have it made. Or why anyone would want to.

As she took a curve to the left, she rolled down

her side window, grabbed the box from him and hefted it out the window.

Stunned, he swung around just in time to see the box explode as it hit the blacktop. Spikes pelted the Buick's windshield. An instant later, the Buick's front tire blew and the car began to rock, then swerve. The Buick hit the ditch in a cloud of dust, burrowing into a small dirt hillside.

"Wow," the kid said. He'd unbuckled his seat belt and now stood looking back as the dust settled over the Buick. "Awesome."

Will pulled Just Zack down and got him buckled in again as Samantha slowed. She smiled down at the boy and gave him a high-five. The kid was grinning from ear to ear. This woman was *not* a good role model.

"I'm Samantha but most people just call me 'Sam.'"

Just Zack turned shy.

"And this is—" her gaze shifted to Will "—Will, an acquaintance of mine."

Passing acquaintance, he thought. What was going on? Why had she grabbed this kid? And who were those men? And more to the point, who was this woman?

He realized he was getting a headache just trying to figure it all out. And what was the point? Obviously, she was all wrong for him.

Absently, he considered what he might be doing right now if he'd listened to his sister's advice. He glanced down at his left wrist to check the time. His watch was gone! How was that possible? He'd just had it.

"My watch—"

"Give it back, Zack," Samantha ordered, not even looking at the boy.

Zack let out a long-suffering sigh, reached into his jacket pocket and extracted the watch.

Samantha snatched it from the kid and handed it to Will. "Sorry. I should have warned you."

Will stared down at the boy, then at Samantha. They both looked so…innocent.

Samantha turned off the highway onto a dirt road.

"There is a good explanation for all of this, right?" he asked, sounding pathetically hopeful. He glanced over at her when she didn't answer.

She no longer had the gun resting on her thighs. The late-afternoon sun slanted into the car, turning the wisps of hair around her face golden as she slowed the Firebird to an almost legal speed and glanced over to meet his gaze.

"There is always an explanation. I'm just not sure it's one you're going to like."

Chapter Three

A fork in the road loomed ahead. Left would take her to the nearest town where she could get rid of Will. Right would put some distance between her and the kidnappers and take her to someplace safe for the night.

Relatively safe, she amended. Being around Will made her feel anything but. He reminded her too much of her girlhood dreams of love, marriage, babies and happily ever after. All the things she didn't want to be reminded of, especially right now. That's why she'd like nothing better than to take Will into town and be done with him.

"Just out of curiosity, how many men have you handcuffed to your dash?" he asked, jerking her from her dilemma.

"Not that many," she said, sounding defensive even to herself. Most males gave her a wide berth. Her mother said it was because she intimidated men. *"Act helpless,"* her mother advised. *"Men like that. Look at your cousin Shelly. Men just flock to help her. Have you ever met a more helpless woman?"*

The truth was, she was no Shelly. She didn't even think she could *act* that helpless.

As she slowed for the fork in the road ahead, she felt Will studying her like a bug in a mason jar.

You should never have kissed him!

Oh? What would you suggest I should have done? Get us both killed?

You could have told him the truth after the kiss.

Oh, come on, give me a break. I thought I was never going to see him again. And anyway, I *liked* the kiss—

"Hello?"

She blinked and glanced over at him. He was looking at her oddly. She stared out over the hood and saw that she'd stopped in the middle of the road at the fork.

"Well?" he asked, looking worried.

She glanced down at Zack. He looked worried, as well. She smiled at him and winked as if to say, *No problem here.* But even as she hit the gas, she wasn't sure she was making the right decision. That alone scared her.

She took the fork to the right, heading for the hills. Will Sheridan be damned. She had to hide out for a while until the dust settled. Until she figured out what was going on. There was little doubt in her mind that something was wrong with this case.

And as for Will—well, he'd just have to cool his heels, too. She still couldn't believe he'd tracked her down— Let alone tracked her down to ask her for a date! Her luck with men definitely wasn't improving.

When he'd first gotten into the Firebird, she'd been so sure it was about her busting the commissioner at his sister's party. Obviously he still didn't realize what she'd been doing there. But when he did—

She glanced over at him. What *would* he do? She'd thought she had him all figured out. Until he climbed into her car and refused to get out. From what she'd learned about the man, *that* was so far out of character that it wasn't even in his solar system anymore.

She eyed him, wondering what had caused such impetuous behavior.

Hello? Remember the way you kissed him at the party?

Come on, one little kiss?

She narrowed her gaze at him. Did she have reason to be concerned about what he'd do next? No, she didn't think she could expect any more surprises out of him. What you saw was what you got: a successful businessman in control of his normal everyday life and happy about it. Except, he didn't look all that happy right now.

She grimaced at the thought, as the Firebird left the pavement and barreled up the narrow dirt road toward the mountains. Out of the corner of her eye, she saw Will's brow shoot up. She ignored his pointed look.

"Why do I get the feeling you're not taking me to the next town where I can get out?"

"We can't go there just yet," she said. "But trust me, I'm as anxious to let you out of this car as you are to get out."

"I highly doubt that."

She groaned inwardly, wishing they could have

met under other circumstances— Who was she kidding? It wouldn't have made any difference. Eventually he'd find out the truth about her, and a man like Will Sheridan wasn't going to take that well.

No reason to think about might-have-beens. She had to deal with now, and that was going to be challenging enough.

WILL LOOKED UP the empty road, at the sun setting behind distant low mountains, the day fading into the horizon. This was all his fault. What kind of fool spotted a woman at a party and followed her out to the patio with two full glasses of champagne, thinking to himself, *This is the woman I'm going to marry?*

He didn't even want to consider what kind of fool would get into her car and refuse to get out.

Just a fool who knew what he wanted and went after it, the consequences be damned. He'd planned his life since before kindergarten, from when to become skilled at the alphabet to what point he should move on to the multiplication tables.

In high school he'd decided he wanted to construct buildings and eventually start his own construction company. He wasn't like his college friends who changed majors four times. Or who, unbelievably, started college not even knowing what they wanted to be.

He couldn't imagine letting life toss him around like a fallen leaf, blowing wherever the breeze took him. He had a plan—from the clothing he wore to the food he ate to the woman he wanted to marry.

So what was he doing handcuffed to the dash of

this woman's Firebird? This had definitely *not* been in his plan.

Worse yet, he'd never been so aware of a woman. Or less happy about it: the faint smell of her perfume, the soft sound of each breath, the warm pulsing air around her.

Not that she was making it easy to ignore her. Especially the way she was dressed. What little her sparse clothing did leave to the imagination, he had no trouble supplying.

But she was all wrong for his bride. That much was obvious. He wanted a woman with a career that at least complemented his. A woman who wanted to bear his children. Not steal someone else's. A woman who didn't carry a gun. Or beat up strange men in broad daylight in front of rest homes. Was he asking too much?

God, I'll bet she hasn't even started a 401K, he thought miserably.

He watched as she drove up a narrow dirt road as if she knew where she was going. He didn't doubt she did.

The road ended high on a mountainside at the bottom of a rock cliff. Through a stand of dark green ponderosa pines, he spotted a house set back against the cliff.

He stared at the small wood-frame house with the two-car attached garage. The place appeared empty, the curtains drawn, no lights glowing behind them in the growing dusk.

Samantha pulled up to the garage door on the left and reached under her seat. He half expected her to come out with a weapon again. Or a crowbar to break into the place. Nothing would have surprised him at that point.

Except a garage-door opener. She hit the button, and the door groaned open, the light coming on inside to reveal a single empty bay separated from the other half of the garage by a wall with a door.

"You live here?" he asked in shock.

She shook her head as she pulled the Firebird into the space and shut off the engine. "It's my cousin's place." She put an arm around Zack. "I would imagine you're hungry."

The boy nodded, unhooked his seat belt and stood again to look out the rear window as if he feared they'd been followed.

"You're safe here, Zack," she said. "Don't worry."

"I'm not worried," he said.

Well, I am, Will thought.

"Come on," she said, opening her car door. "There should be food in the house." She started to climb out.

The rattle of handcuffs seemed to stop her. Will felt her gaze finally slide to his. Her look said she didn't know what to do with him.

He jangled the cuffs and glared at her, more angry with himself than with her. He was the one who'd foolhardily gotten into her car, the one who'd been determined to get a date with her at any cost. Little had he known.

"Sorry." She dug into the glove box, came up with the key and handed it to him. Why hadn't he thought to look in there? Because he'd been too engrossed in this woman's outlandish activities. Awkwardly, he unlocked the cuffs, not looking at her.

"I hate to tell you, but we need to stay here for the night," she said. "In the morning, I'll take you to town and rent you a car. I'm afraid that's the best I can do. I have my reasons."

He was sure she did. And he didn't want to know them. Under normal circumstances, he'd have called a taxi. Or demanded she take him now to the nearest town.

But he doubted it was as simple as demanding she take him anywhere. Or calling a taxi. He wasn't even sure where they were or how far it was to the next town.

And he *had* gotten himself into this.

"Fine," he said. "But I can rent my own car." He handed her the cuffs and key, and she and the boy got out. What was one night? But as she opened the Firebird's trunk and took out her overnight bag, he reminded himself to watch her more closely should she ever kiss him again.

She put an arm around the boy as she opened the door to the house and ushered him in.

Will followed, not surprised to find the house compact, the decor simple, practical and very male. The air inside was cold and a little musty, as if whoever lived here hadn't been around for a while.

"Would you mind building a fire while I change, and then I'll scare us up some food?" she asked as she headed for what appeared to be the smaller of the bedrooms. "There're split logs out back. I'm sure Zack will help you."

SAMANTHA DIDN'T WAIT for an answer, just hurried off to get into less revealing clothing. From her bag, she took out jeans and a cable-knit Irish wool sweater. She caught her reflection in the mirror on the back wall and froze. Most of her hair had come out of the ponytail and now hung around her face in curls. She pulled out the scrunchie and ran her fingers through her hair, not wanting to take the time to find a brush.

The truth was, she didn't want to look as if she'd been primping. Or that she might be interested in Will Sheridan. It was obvious he wouldn't be asking her for a date when she dropped him off at the first town in the morning. This time, she knew she wouldn't be seeing him again. Once more she couldn't help feeling disappointed—and relieved. He was all wrong for her, anyway.

She headed for the kitchen and quickly busied herself making dinner, as she listened to Zack and Will bring in wood.

Moments later, Zack appeared in the doorway. "Can I play a game on the computer?" he asked.

She glanced down at him, shocked suddenly by how small and vulnerable he looked. She wanted to take him in her arms and reassure him. But she could feel the wall the little boy had built around him, and knew that sometimes such walls were all that kept a person standing.

She knelt down and gently touched his shoulder. "Of course, you can. Do you need help?"

He shook his head.

"Zack, I knew your mom and dad in college,"

she said. "Your mom's the one who hired me to find
you."

He nodded as if none of that mattered. "Can I play
the games now?"

"Sure."

A few minutes later she heard the distinct sound
of a computer game coming from the other room.
She'd never been much of a computer-game person,
but her cousin Charley who lived out on the West
Coast could play for hours.

She peeked around the doorjamb. Will crouched
in front of the woodstove. Not far away, Zack was
on his knees in the chair in front of the computer,
his small dark head silhouetted against the screen,
reminding her of his father. A wave of regret washed
over her, weighing down her heart. She hurriedly
turned back to her cooking.

Soon the sound of the crackling fire in the woodstove and the faint hint of pine smoke drifted into
the kitchen—along with Will.

He seemed to set the air around her in motion as
he leaned against the wall beside the stove and
watched, his arms folded across his chest, a frown
on his handsome face.

"Who are you?" he asked.

She'd been expecting this. And dreading it. Obviously he'd gotten the wrong impression at his sister's party. She hated to disappoint him further.

"My name *is* Samantha. Samantha—" she shot
him a sheepish look "—Murphy."

He nodded as if not surprised that she'd lied to
him. She could see herself drop another notch in his
eyes. At this rate she'd reach bottom in no time.

"I'm a private investigator."

He sighed. That obviously wasn't what he'd been hoping for, either. "You have some ID, I assume?"

She retrieved her purse from the bedroom and handed him both her driver's license and private investigator's ID.

He glanced at them, then at her, then handed them back. "Butte?"

She nodded, biting her tongue not to add, *Want to make something of it?* Butte wasn't exactly considered scenic Montana, but she liked the old mining city, even with its open pit and its reputation as the "butte" of jokes.

"And the party?" he asked simply.

"I was on a job." She waited for him to put two and two together. But he didn't seem interested in what she'd been doing there.

"And the kiss?" he asked, getting to the heart of it.

She took a breath, reluctant to tell him that she'd used him as cover. "I liked it," she said, unconsciously licking her upper lip. "A lot."

His chuckle was short on humor. "I wasn't asking for a rating."

She turned away to dump a can of broth into the pot on the stove. *Just get it over with, once and for all.* "Okay, I used you. You came along at just the right time. You were cover."

"COVER?" His ego went down to the mat for a ten-count.

She mugged an apologetic face over her shoulder. "I never thought I'd see you again."

Obviously. "Well, I think that *covers* that." It just kept getting better. He stared at her, her back straight, shoulders tensed as if she were anticipating a blow.

She'd taken her hair out of the ponytail. It fell around her shoulders in golden waves, the same color as the freckles across the bridge of her nose.

He reminded himself that this woman had fooled him. True, the only real lie she'd told him was her name the night of the party. He wasn't sure a "kiss for cover" constituted a lie. Possibly.

Everything else about her he'd made up himself. Because he'd wanted her to be the woman he thought she was. What a fool.

"Zack was kidnapped," she said, when he didn't ask.

Will told himself he didn't really want to hear this. The less he knew, the better.

"I was hired to bring him back with the least amount of fanfare."

He stared at her. "In other words, without the authorities knowing anything about it?"

"Something like that."

Her evasiveness made him suspect there was a whole lot more he didn't want to know.

He'd seen this sort of thing on late-night TV. People who specialized in stealing back children. Usually, though, the kidnapper was the parent who'd been denied custody. And the private investigator— Well, none of them looked like Samantha Murphy, that was for sure.

"And your plan?" he enquired against his better judgment. Mostly, he just wanted her to *have* a plan. Any plan. Just some common ground between them.

"Get him back to Seattle as quickly and safely as possible."

He eyed her askance. "That's it?"

She shrugged. "It's the best one I have right now."

It was obvious she went through life flying by the seat of her pants. And although she had one very fine seat, the whole concept appalled him.

"What if those two guys show up again?" he persisted.

"It's unlikely they will, but I really didn't expect them to chase us in the first place," she said, and frowned. "Kidnappers routinely run the other way."

He supposed she should know. "But still—"

"I've found you can't really plan for most things, anyway."

He would have argued that point twenty-four hours ago. Now he just studied her, wondering about the note of regret in her voice. He wondered who had let her down. Probably a man.

He knew he wasn't getting the whole story. About the kidnapping. About Samantha. He hated to think just how much more there *was* to the story. And to this woman. He felt as if he'd only skimmed the surface, and that was terrifying enough.

"Why you and not the police?"

She dropped her gaze. "It's complicated."

He'd just bet it was. He reminded himself he didn't *want* the whole story. But it did make him wonder. Who was he kidding? Everything about this woman made him wonder, when he *should* be concentrating on how he was going to get back to his own life. His birthday was rapidly approaching, and he hadn't found what he was looking for yet.

Well, not exactly.

He watched her cook for a moment, liking the image she made. "What about the boy's family?" he asked, unable not to. Zack had said the men who'd kidnapped him claimed they were friends of his "birth mother." Odd words coming out of the mouth of a five-year-old.

She took a breath. "In a nutshell? He's been living with his father in Seattle. There was a burglary at the computer company where Lucas worked. Now Lucas is missing and wanted for questioning by the police. Zack was at a friend's house when he was abducted."

"Where's his mother?"

She stirred at the pot on the stove. "Cassie?"

He raised a brow. "How many mothers does the kid have?"

"Just Cassie, his birth mother who left when he was a baby, and his ex-stepmother Mercedes, who left after less than a year of marriage."

This could explain the kid's budding criminal career. It sounded as if the boy had been left more times than a Greyhound bus station. Will felt bad for him, knowing what that kind of instability did to a kid.

Well, at least Zack had Samantha now. And as unconventional as her methods were, she'd obviously go to any extreme to keep the boy safe.

But Will still couldn't help worrying about her and the kid. "Is it just me, or isn't it a little strange that first you have the burglary at the computer company where the father works, then the father's disappearance, then the son's kidnapping? And where do the kidnappers take the kid? To a rest home in Wolf Point, Montana.''

She wiped her hands on the apron around her waist and looked over at him. ''Like I said, it's complicated.''

''Right.'' And none of his business. ''What can I do to help with dinner?''

He followed her sudden glance to the doorway. Zack was peering around the door frame, looking as sweet and innocent as any child Will had ever seen. Except, it was obvious the kid had been eavesdropping, hovering there long enough to hear most—if not all—of their conversation.

He checked to make sure he still had his watch. And his wallet.

''We were just talking about the men who abducted you,'' she said, no doubt assuming, as he did, that Zack had been listening for some time. ''Do you have any ideas why they did that?''

Zack shrugged.

''Not a clue, huh?'' she persisted. ''What about your dad? Any ideas where he might be?''

He shook his head and looked away. ''Is dinner almost ready?''

She eyed the boy but didn't push it. ''Just about. Why don't you help Will set the table.'' She glanced in Will's direction for consent.

Will realized he was hungry. Whatever she'd cooked up smelled wonderful. ''Just point us to the dishes.''

They ate a surprisingly delicious casserole at the

kitchen table. He was a little in awe of her ability to throw something this good together so quickly and with only a few ingredients. The woman did seem to have some burgeoning spousal talents. It was her other talents that concerned him.

Zack ate without a word, nodding or shaking his head when Samantha tried to draw him into a conversation. Finally she gave up.

After dinner and dishes, Will went into the living room while she put the boy to bed.

Leaving the bedroom door ajar, she joined him in front of the fire. He'd been staring into the flames when she approached. He found himself still very aware of her. And very curious. More curious than he should have been, considering she didn't fit into his plans.

"How did you get into a profession like this?" he asked, still wishing she did anything else.

She warmed her hands in front of the fire, her gaze on the flames. The light played on her face. She really was beautiful in an innocent, wholesome sort of way. The irony of it didn't escape him.

"My father and uncle and some of my cousins are cops, some others are private investigators." She shrugged. "It was that or become a mortician."

He knew she was joking, but a mortician sounded good to him right now. He watched her glance toward Zack's bedroom, and saw the worry in the little furrow between her brows, in the slope of her strong shoulders, in the depths of her bottomless blue-green gaze. He warned himself to stay out of it.

He'd interfered enough just getting into her Firebird, refusing to get out and asking a lot of questions.

Samantha knew what she was doing. She did this sort of thing all the time, right? And the kid, well, she'd find the boy's father. Or get Zack to one of his mothers.

Tomorrow, as soon as they found a car rental agency, airport or bus station, Will would be returning to his well-planned, safe and simple life. And his quest for a bride. He doubted his path would ever cross Samantha's again, and wondered why it had even once, let alone twice.

His gaze fell on her face, and he felt that same strong pull he had at the party. What was it about this woman that tugged at him like a hangman's noose?

Before he could stop himself, he took her shoulders in his hands and pulled her to him. This time the kiss was all his idea. And a bad one at that. Her lips parted, and she leaned into him as if drawn by a force of her own. He drew her closer, tasting her, teasing her tongue with his, feasting on her luscious inviting mouth, taking but wanting more. So much more.

She pulled back first, her eyes dark with desire. And quiet despair. She didn't have to say a word. They both knew how impossible this was.

He reminded himself that his birthday was only days away. Just the thought of his self-imposed deadline to find a prospective mate made him grit his teeth. He should be out looking. Not kissing this shamus/child-napper.

"We should get some sleep," she said. "We leave early in the morning."

"I'll take the couch," he said hoarsely. There was

only one other bedroom aside from the one Zack was in.

She didn't put up an argument. Probably decided to let him have a little control over his life. How thoughtful. She got him some bedding and then bid him good-night, disappearing into the second bedroom but leaving the door ajar.

He stood before the fire for a long time, staring into the flames, feeling anxious and wide-awake, the kiss still coursing through him like high-voltage electricity, giving him a buzz, making him jittery.

After a while, the fire burned down and his heart rate slowed. The fire inside him cooled. He returned to his usual sensible self again, and went to look in on Zack.

The little boy was out, a slight smile on his cherub face. The kid *was* cute. He had his arm around his backpack as if everything he cared about was inside. Will wondered if that was true. What had this boy's life been like? And how had he become such an adept thief at such a young age?

Will smiled wryly, remembering his own childhood. He wondered if he didn't have more in common with Zackarias Lucien O'Brien than anyone would have suspected.

He left the bedroom door partially open and glanced into the other bedroom. Samantha was curled in a fetal position, the covers kicked off. He stepped in and quietly pulled the quilt up over her slim frame. In slumber, she had Zack's childlike angelic sweetness about her.

Unless you noticed the barrel of her pistol sticking out from under her pillow.

Chapter Four

Samantha woke just before daybreak, the dream so real she jumped out of bed, her heart pounding, and rushed in to check on Zack.

Curled in the middle of the double bed, he looked even smaller and more vulnerable than usual. She felt her breath catch at the sight of his tiny sleeping form. So young. So alone. So scared.

She knew how he felt. Since the night of the party, her life had been thrown into spin cycle. Lucas missing, suspected of a burglary at the computer company where he'd worked. The police looking for him. Zack kidnapped. And her house ransacked.

She thought about the kidnappers and what Will had said about them taking the boy to the rest home. It didn't make any sense. Unless you knew Lucas.

So why hadn't he called again? She'd been so sure he would. From the moment Cassie had contacted her, Samantha had believed Lucas was behind Zack's so-called kidnapping, just as Cassie had. She'd been convinced of it when she'd learned from her cousin Charley, the cop, that Lucas had purchased two train tickets to Wolf Point. She hadn't been surprised when she'd found the kidnappers had taken Zack to Wolf Point to his great-grandmother's rest home.

That theory began to unravel when Lucas didn't show up; when she found out that Lucas's grandmother, Gladdie O'Brien, had Alzheimer's and didn't know anyone, including Lucas, and hadn't for months. But Samantha hadn't gotten worried until the kidnappers had chased her after she'd snatched Zack. They hadn't looked like friends of Lucas's. They'd looked like thugs, not computer geeks.

Maybe the train tickets had been a red herring, and Cassie was wrong about Lucas setting up the kidnapping. But why would anyone else kidnap Zack? What had the kidnappers hoped to accomplish? And, just as Will had noted, why take the boy to Wolf Point, Montana, to a rest home? Why no ransom demand?

When Lucas hadn't shown up by the second time the kidnappers took Zack to the rest home, Sam had known she had to act—and quickly. She'd left a message with the head nurse for Lucas to call her on her cell phone, and she'd grabbed Zack from the kidnappers.

She'd counted on Lucas calling, convinced he was alive and had set this up to be with his son. But if that were true, then where was he? Why hadn't he called? Maybe something had detained him or— She didn't like to consider the alternative. That something had happened to him.

But if she was wrong about the kidnapping, then maybe she was wrong about why the kidnappers had taken Zack to the rest home. Were they looking for

Lucas for another reason aside from giving him his son? Or were they looking for something else?

She closed her eyes, her head aching. There was only one thing she could be sure of: Lucas loved his son and wouldn't have left him unless he had to. She knew Lucas.

She leaned down to brush a lock of hair back from the boy's face, feeling a surge of affection so strong it almost dropped her to her knees. This child could have been hers. Should have been hers.

Those kinds of thoughts got her nowhere, she reminded herself. Instead she needed to concentrate on getting Zack safely to Seattle. Then what? Ideally, Lucas would turn up with a good explanation for his disappearance.

But she wasn't counting on that. Cassie had hinted that Lucas might be in some sort of trouble. If she wanted answers, she'd have to get them from Cassie. Or Zack. She suspected the boy knew as much as anyone about what was going on. But for some reason, he was either afraid or unwilling to tell her.

When she'd questioned him last night, he'd definitely seemed frightened. But why wouldn't he be? His father was missing and strangers had kidnapped him. That would be enough to scare any kid.

She shook her head. Normally, she operated on instinct. But now her instincts were telling her they couldn't be trusted. She was too personally involved. Add to that Will Sheridan. No wonder she was having nightmares.

As she turned to leave the room, she caught sight of Will, his long lean male body stretched the length of the couch in the living room. He'd also been in her dream. Her skin flushed at the memory. That part of the dream had left her aching, just as his kiss had.

Irritably she quickly showered and dressed, then dialed the Lazy Rest. No one had called for Gladdie O'Brien. Nor had Lucas O'Brien come by. She hung up and headed for the kitchen.

Cooking. It was the one activity that could get her mind off everything else. Usually. Unless the object of her distraction was visible through the doorway.

What had that kiss of his been about last night? Payback?

She began to beat up a coffee cake, banging the pan, thinking about men. Thinking about the one in the living room, in particular.

WILL WOKE to the banging of pots and pans. He sat up, startled and confused. It took him a moment to remember where he was. And why. He groaned and fell back onto the couch with thoughts of pulling the covers over his head and going back to sleep.

But Samantha wasn't having any of that. The noise in the kitchen grew louder. He peeked over the back of the couch and saw her slamming around, looking out of sorts. What had made him think he'd want to wake up to that face every morning?

He got up and padded barefoot into the kitchen, noticing his clothing looked like he'd slept in it. He had. It was something he'd never imagined himself doing—before yesterday.

''Anything I can do to help?'' he asked from directly behind her.

She let out a satisfying yelp of surprise and dropped one of the pans.

He picked it up and handed it to her. "Sleep well?" he enquired. She smelled heavenly, her hair still damp, her skin glowing.

"Not as well as you, it appears."

He actually felt pretty good, considering the couch had been a little short for him and he'd had trouble getting to sleep after the kiss. But once he'd drifted off, he'd slept wonderfully, although too briefly. "Must have been the mountain air."

"Humph," she said.

He watched her, perversely enjoying the thought that their kiss might have disturbed her sleep. Her kiss at the party certainly had more than disturbed *him.*

He knew it wasn't fair to blame her because she hadn't turned out to be the woman he'd thought she was. But he couldn't help himself. She'd definitely looked the part at the party. But that had been the point, hadn't it? To fool people? Well, she'd fooled him, all right.

He caught a whiff of the intriguing scents emanating from the oven and was again reminded of her culinary skills—although he did wonder what she'd done with her gun.

As the coffeemaker finished, he helped himself to a cup and poured one for her, as well.

She took it almost contritely. "Thanks." Her gaze touched his, and he saw something in her eyes that surprised him. Fear.

"Wanna talk about it?"

She shook her head and turned her back to him as she continued making breakfast. "I'm just worried about Zack's father."

He stepped around to her side so he could see her profile. "He hasn't turned up?"

She shook her head again. "I'd hoped he would by now."

He nodded, wanting to cup her face in his hands and kiss away her fears. But her fears were real, and his kisses only had the power to make matters worse. Ultimately, he was heading back to Billings. Samantha to Seattle and whatever awaited her there, then back to Butte. They'd made their choices a long time ago.

"Something sure smells good," he said.

She gave him a small smile, acknowledging his change of subject. "I just whipped up a coffee cake and a frittata. If you'd get down the plates—"

"You've got it." He passed close enough to her in the small kitchen that he could feel her body heat. She seemed to radiate a sensual warmth that drew him more powerfully than gravity. He hurriedly set the table.

"My cousin's about your size," she said.

He looked up and realized she'd caught him inspecting his wrinkled linen slacks.

"I can scare you up some clean clothes, and there're fresh towels in the bathroom," she said.

Under normal circumstances he wouldn't have borrowed clothing. Especially from Samantha's cousin. If that was who really owned the place. But just the thought of a shower and clean clothes sounded so...normal.

He took a hot shower, letting the water pour over him the way thoughts of Samantha did. He felt anxious, too aware of the woman in the next room, too aware of his desire for her. He unconsciously made a mental list, which, of course, ended heavily weighted on the con side. What was he doing? He knew she wasn't what he was looking for. No reason to flog a dead horse.

When he stepped out of the shower, he found clean jeans, a T-shirt, socks, boxers and a shirt waiting for him. The thought that she'd come in while he was in the shower did nothing to curb his longing. An image of the two of them in the tub together, soapy and pink from the heat, flashed into his head. He groaned, turned on the cold water in the shower and stepped back in.

When he got out again, he heard the cell phone ring and Samantha answer it. Quietly, he cracked open the bathroom door, shocked that he was eavesdropping.

Worse yet, that he was letting himself be drawn deeper into this—whatever it was. He was too intrigued with "Sam" Murphy and too worried about her little pickpocket ward.

"I've been trying to reach you," Sam said, unable to keep the admonition out of her voice. It had been two days since she'd gotten the frantic call from Cassie about Zack's kidnapping. Two days and no word since, although she'd left messages at the number Cassie had given her. The number, it turned out, was an answering service in Seattle.

"Have you heard from Lucas?"

"Nothing," Cassie said. "The police are still looking for him in connection with the burglary at Whiz Kidz."

"Whiz Kidz?" she asked.

"Lucas's computer software company."

Wait a minute. "Lucas *owns* the company?"

"He is one of the partners. Did you find Zack?"

The hope in Cassie's voice touched her more than she wanted to admit. "He's with me."

"Thank God."

Cassie sounded so relieved. Maybe she genuinely did care about her son.

"You were right. The kidnappers went to Wolf Point to Lucas's grandmother."

"Had Gladdie heard from Lucas?" Cassie asked anxiously.

So Cassie didn't know. "Gladdie O'Brien's in a nursing home. She has Alzheimer's and doesn't even remember she has a grandson named Lucas."

"Oh, no."

Cassie sounded upset. Had she known Gladdie well? Sam assumed so, since Gladdie was Lucas's closest relative. *Only* relative, as far as Sam knew.

"So that means if Lucas had tried to contact her—"

"The head nurse said Lucas hasn't called or been to see Gladdie in several months," Samantha broke in.

"Really?" Cassie said. "Lucas hadn't even written her? Or sent her anything?"

The question struck Sam as odd. *Sent her anything?* "Like what?"

"I don't know, a card or a package. I think she just had a birthday. It's not like Lucas to forget it. They were very close."

"I'm sure the head nurse would have mentioned

a letter or a package," Sam said. "But Gladdie wouldn't even know who it was from."

"I suppose you're right. But at least you have Zack."

She thought of what Will had said the night before. "I'm curious. What made you think the kidnappers would take Zack to his great-grandmother's?"

"I just thought Lucas would want to see her before he left the country."

"Lucas was leaving the country?"

"It's just an expression, Sam. I mean, if he was on the run—"

"Cassie, what's going on? You know, Zack told me that the men who took him said they were friends of *yours*."

"That's crazy," Cassie snapped. "The kidnappers must have been trying to get him to trust them so he'd go with them quietly."

"Wouldn't it have made a lot more sense to tell him they were friends of his *father,* since Zack doesn't even know you?"

"I swear to you, Sam, I *don't* know. Unless they meant Mercedes."

"Mercedes?" Mercedes had been Cassie's sorority sister for a short stint and Lucas's second wife for an even shorter stint, further proving he continued to marry the wrong women.

"What does Mercedes have to do with this?" she asked.

"Maybe nothing. I just know they went through a divorce. Mercedes blamed Zack for coming between them because he never liked her and Lucas knew it."

Sam cursed herself for getting involved in this.

Again. It hadn't been that long ago that she'd been mentally planning a fairy tale wedding with Lucas. Mrs. Samantha O'Brien.

She closed her eyes, the pain still sharp, the ache still there, the loss staggering. She'd lost so much more than Lucas.

And now she'd let Lucas and Cassie drag her back into the past and all the hurt and regrets that came with it. She should wash her hands of this whole mess right now.

She thought of the little boy in the next room and opened her eyes. Cassie might have hired her, but neither she nor Lucas was why Sam had taken the case. She'd started out doing it for Lucas, but the reason she was staying in the case was for Zack, the little boy she'd once dreamed of having with Lucas. It wasn't Zack's fault his birth mother was a flake and his father knew more about computers than women. *Or kids,* she thought, remembering Zack's propensity for pickpocketing.

"Cassie, what kind of trouble is Lucas in?"

"Did I say he was in trouble?"

"Give me a break," she snapped. "What's going on?"

"It's…complicated."

Sam groaned inwardly, thinking how she'd used those same evasive words with Will. "Uncomplicate it for me then."

Cassie seemed to hesitate. "I talked to Lucas a few weeks ago. He was upset. He thought someone was trying to steal his latest game design." She sounded skeptical. "He said he was worried about Zack."

That would explain the strange phone call.

"Sam, I think he might have set this all up—the burglary, his disappearance, all of it."

"Why?" she asked in disbelief.

"Maybe to get out of some debts he owed," Cassie said.

"Would he do that?" Not the Lucas she had fallen in love with at college. But did that man still exist? Or had he ever existed?

"Maybe."

"Cassie, it's obvious you know something. Tell me what the hell is going on."

Silence, then a whisper. "Not on the phone. Meet me somewhere. I really need to see Zack, anyway. Just so I can see with my own eyes that he's all right. You know what I mean? I think it would be best if he doesn't see me, though. Or, at least, doesn't know who I am—" Her voice broke. "Do you think that's possible? I could tell you everything then."

Samantha didn't relish the idea of seeing Cassie. She still harbored hard feelings toward her former roommate, and seeing the woman would only bring back painful memories. But she couldn't ignore the pain she heard in Cassie's voice, either.

Still, if the woman cared so much about her son, why had she left him? How could she have given up her child like that?

"Cassie—"

"Please, Sam."

She heard tears in Cassie's voice. Real or not, they affected her. And she did need answers. Why Cassie had them was another question altogether.

"You're in Seattle, right?"

"No, I'm in Butte. I just assumed you'd come back here first, before you headed for Seattle."

Samantha felt her heart begin to pound.

"I could meet you at your office," Cassie was saying. "Or your house."

Cassie knew Samantha had a house? The same house that had been ransacked three nights ago? She felt a chill slog through her veins. "No, that wouldn't be a good place to meet. I had to grab Zack right in front of the rest home. By now the police are probably looking for me." She hoped that was a lie.

If she had to meet Cassie somewhere, she wanted it to be in a public place. She'd be carrying a lot of baggage from the past and she wanted their meeting to be as quick and painless as possible. She also wanted Zack and Will where she could see them. And she couldn't be sure the kidnappers weren't waiting for her at her house. Or her office.

"We could meet at the Butte mall."

"The mall?" Cassie sounded a little surprised.

"In the food court."

"You'll have Zack with you?" she asked anxiously.

"Yes. He'll be with me."

"I can't tell you how much this means to me."

Was it possible that Cassie really did love Zack? Had she known she'd make a terrible mother and that's why she left Zack and Lucas?

"Just tell me when to be there," Cassie said.

Samantha glanced at her watch. She was more than four hundred miles away. "I could be there by eight."

"Eight?" Cassie paused. "Eight will be fine. The

mall won't be real busy at that hour. I'll see you there. If anything should happen, I'll stop by your office.'' Cassie hung up—but not before Sam heard another voice in the background. A man's voice. Lucas?

What had she meant, *if anything should happen?*

She snapped off the phone with an unladylike curse. Every instinct in her cried, *Turn Zack over to the authorities.* Let them sort this out. Don't get any more involved than you already are. There is something terribly wrong with this whole mess.

But even as she thought it, she knew she couldn't. If she went to the cops now, they'd turn Zack over to Cassie until Lucas could be found. And after all these years, Cassie suddenly wanted to see her son a little too desperately. Why was that?

"Is everything all right?" Will asked as he came out of the bathroom. His frown indicated he'd at least heard her colorful curse. Maybe more.

"Fine," she fibbed. "I'll get Zack. We'd better eat, and then get going."

Reviewing the too-brief, disturbing telephone conversation, she fell upon the two things she knew. Cassie had sounded anxious—anxious to see Zack. And a little scared. Samantha shivered. What was it Cassie wasn't telling her? Something about Lucas? And why did Samantha fear it was something she didn't want to hear?

In the bedroom, Sam woke Zack and got him dressed. He slipped on the backpack, hugged his CD player to him, and tugged the headphones up over his ears under his cap, now-familiar music leaking out.

She gently slipped the headphones from his ears. "We need to talk," she said, and led him out to the living room. He perched on the edge of the couch, and she sat down across from him. He looked wary.

"Zack, I need your help. I have to know what's going on so I can find your dad and keep you safe. If you know anything about your dad or the two men who took you or why, please tell me now."

He stared at her, his eyes dark, but still he said nothing.

"Are you afraid they'll come after you again?"

He shook his head, but not very convincingly.

"I wouldn't let them take you."

He eyed her skeptically.

"Come on, I got you away from them, didn't I? And I lost them when they tried to chase us, didn't I?"

He smiled a little. "Yeah."

"So have some faith. I have a few more tricks up my sleeve."

He seemed to accept that she just might. Out of the corner of her eye, she saw Will. He didn't seem as happy to hear about the tricks up her sleeve.

"They didn't hurt you, did they?" she asked, trying a different tack.

"No," he said quickly. "They were okay."

"What did they feed you?" she asked, having already witnessed at dinner his fondness for food.

His eyes lit as he recited a list of junk foods from quarter-pounders to pizza pockets. "...and cinnamon rolls and cookies and popcorn."

Geez, he'd eaten enough to bankrupt the kidnappers. But there had been no ransom note. With Lucas missing, where would they have sent one?

"Then they fed you all right," she said.

"Oh yeah," he said enthusiastically. "They let me have anything I wanted, and they had really cool stuff."

"Where were they taking you when I came along?"

He shrugged.

"You never overheard them talking about what they were going to do or why?"

"They didn't say much of anything."

Why didn't she believe that?

She could feel Will's gaze on her. She hadn't been completely honest with him when he'd asked about her plans yesterday. Those plans were a little more complex than just getting Zack to Seattle.

She tried a different approach. "What about their names. They did call each other by name, right?"

He seemed to think about that for a moment. "Al."

"Which one was that?"

"The real nice little one."

"And the larger of the two?"

Zack studied the rug. "Ralph."

Al and Ralph? She watched his face, wondering if he was lying and what reason he'd have to do so. Did he want to protect his kidnappers? She remembered how easily he'd come with her when she'd abducted him. She had a feeling that he'd been handed off to a lot of people in his young life.

"Had you ever seen the men before?"

Zack shook his head. Samantha glanced over at

Will. He was frowning slightly, but she knew that might not have anything to do with the boy's story. He'd been frowning a lot since he'd gotten into her car yesterday.

But he'd be gone soon. With the first bus station, airport or car rental agency they saw.

She looked at Zack again, wanting to ask him more but realizing it wouldn't do any good. They had some time before they reached Butte. Maybe he'd open up when the two of them were alone.

She just hoped she could win his trust before it was too late. Because she had a bad feeling about what was waiting for them up the road.

Chapter Five

"We won't be taking the Firebird."

Will stopped in the garage doorway to look back at Samantha. She wore jeans and a shirt, the top open, exposing just a hint of freckled chest. After having seen her attire yesterday, he felt as if he already knew her body fairly well. But as she stepped past him and into the garage—the jeans molding her bottom, the shirt flashing just a hint of tanned bare skin—he felt as if everything about her was a mystery he needed to solve. Wanted to solve.

"We're not taking the Firebird?" he asked, suddenly worried.

He and Zack hung back as she opened the second garage stall. In the darkness inside, he glimpsed a glint of chrome. A few moments later an engine turned over, and she backed out in their new ride.

Unable to let go of his first erroneous impression of the woman, he'd been rather hoping for a Lexus or a Camry or an Accord. No such luck.

The black Bronco she drove out of the garage made him nervous. It had oversize, nubby, off-road tires, sounded souped up, and made him fear that they'd be needing its four-wheel drive capabilities before they reached the next town.

Reluctantly, he opened the rear door of the Bronco for Zack and waited while the boy and his backpack got in.

"I liked your other car," Zack grumbled as he buckled up.

"Maybe it's cooler than you think," she said cryptically. "You'll see."

Will hoped not. If they needed the Bronco's "special powers," they'd be in some sort of trouble again. Being on the run wasn't in his life's blueprint.

And he knew they wouldn't be switching cars if Samantha wasn't worried. The thought definitely made him anxious.

As he climbed into the front seat, he looked back at Zack. The kid's headphones were on, his baseball cap pulled low, that uninterested somewhere-else look in his eyes again. Will wondered if the boy's kidnappers had fallen for it. He had a feeling they'd probably underestimated this kid.

After what he'd overheard of Samantha's phone call with Zack's birth mother this morning, he was all the more curious about the kid. And Samantha. What role did she play in all this?

From what he could gather from the conversation, Cassie had hired Samantha to get Zack and had known somehow that the kidnappers had taken Zack to the rest home in Wolf Point. Lucas owned a company called Whiz Kidz and was in some sort of trouble that might involve his ex-wife Mercedes.

He was more confused than ever. But it sounded as if Samantha planned to meet Cassie in Butte and get some answers. He didn't trust Cassie and didn't think Samantha should, either. He didn't like the idea, but reminded himself it wasn't any of his business.

Samantha drove in silence, winding the Bronco down the narrow dirt to the stretch of straight blacktop that pointed west like an arrow. There was little traffic at this time of the morning. It felt as if they were the only people left on the planet.

Zack fell asleep only a few miles down the road. Will slipped the headphones from the boy's ears and tried to make him comfortable. Zack stirred awake just long enough to hug his backpack snugly, then dozed off again, his breathing rhythmic, his eyelids fluttering like butterflies as he dreamed.

"There's something in his backpack," Will whispered conspiratorially to Samantha.

She looked over at him in obvious surprise. "What do you mean, 'something'?"

He shook his head, not wanting to let on that he'd listened in on her phone conversation. "Something. Something he's real protective of. Haven't you noticed? He hasn't let that backpack out of his sight. He even sleeps with it."

Her look said she'd noticed. She seemed to study Will, probably wondering why he should care. After today, he'd never see either of them again.

"Thanks. I'll take a look."

For an instant, her gaze locked with his. The air inside the Bronco seemed to compact. Suddenly it felt too close, too confined, way too intimate. The engine throbbed. His heart rate felt in sync with its powerful beat.

Then she broke the connection, looked back to the highway.

He listened to the hum of the tires on the blacktop and watched the early cold morning rush by like wisps of fog. Slowly, he released his held breath. Next to him, he thought he heard her let out a similar sigh.

They passed through one small sleeping community after another. Hinsdale. Saco. Sleeping Buffalo. By the time the sun had come up and filled the Bronco with some warmth, Zack was awake and complaining he was hungry, although he'd eaten two huge pieces of coffee cake, a large glass of milk and a banana before they'd left.

Samantha laughed as she slowed for the town squatting on the flat horizon: Malta, Montana. Home of the Mustangs, and the first town that looked as if it might be large enough to at least have a bus station.

"I'm hungry," Zack groaned sleepily from the back seat.

"You must have a bottomless stomach or a hollow leg," she joked. "As soon as we drop Will off so he can get back to Wolf Point, I'll get you something to eat."

"There's a place—" the boy cried. "I'm *real* hungry. I need a hamburger. And some fries. And a vanilla milk shake. No, make it chocolate."

"Zack, it's eight in the morning!" she shot back.

"Go ahead and feed him first," Will told her.

"Are you sure?" she asked, glancing over.

Her eyes were that warm tropical blue-green in the morning sunlight and her freckles were like gold dust on her nose and cheekbones. He nodded. Once Zack was fed, Samantha could continue on to Seattle via the Butte mall.

And Will would go home.

But he wasn't quite ready yet to tell them goodbye, and the silent admission didn't please him. The one-sided conversation he'd overheard between Samantha and Zack's birth mother had left him with a bad feeling he couldn't quite shake. He feared Samantha had gotten into more than she could handle.

As SAM PARKED in the large lot at the rear of a café that served burgers twenty-four hours a day, she felt a chill on her neck. She glanced around. They were miles from where she'd seen the kidnappers go off the road yesterday, were now driving a different rig, and she hadn't seen any sign of a tail.

Still, she felt uneasy. Much different from the way Will Sheridan made her feel. And oh lordy, how he made her *feel*.

"What about you? You up for a burger, fries and a shake?" she asked, her voice sounding a lot lighter than she felt. "Or are you a ham and eggs and hash browns kind of guy?"

She doubted Will Sheridan had ever had a hamburger, fries and a shake at eight in the morning in his life. No more than he'd ever been handcuffed to a Firebird's dash before. Well, at least he'd never get into a strange car again. Let alone refuse to get out. Something about that made her sad because she knew he'd also be more careful about the next woman he asked out.

She hated what she'd done to him and wished there was something she could do or say to make it

up to him. Dangerous thinking. Even more dangerous, she almost wished she were the woman he'd first
thought she was.

She realized she had been once. A long time ago.
Before Lucas and Cassie and Zack.

"I'd have a little something to eat," Will said.

"Great." She didn't feel the least bit hungry, but
if Zack was— He seemed small for his age. She definitely didn't want him to go hungry.

As she slid into a booth with Zack, she could hear
faint music coming from his CD player. He had his
cap pulled low, his ears protruding, those damn headphones like a wall between him and the outside
world.

She reached over and tugged one side of the headphones down. "Not in the restaurant," she mouthed.

He nodded reluctantly but did as he was told.

"Put the CD player in your backpack," she said,
wondering how she would ever get close to the boy.
Or if she would.

In the end, she ordered what Zack did: a cheese-
burger loaded, fries and a chocolate shake. To her
amazement, so did Will.

"Living dangerously?" she joked, and could have
bitten her tongue when his gaze came up to meet
hers.

"Definitely," he said, his look blistering.

WILL CURSED the chemistry that arced across the
worn Formica table between them. His attraction to
this woman bothered him. He was much too sensible
to let himself fall for the wrong woman. A woman
who was a complete mystery to him. Who could turn

him inside out and disrupt the world he'd made for himself. What did he really know about her, other than the fact that she kissed wonderfully, was a private investigator in Butte, and stole children?

He watched her drag her gaze away, her teeth worrying at her lower lip as she looked out the window. He'd seen her scanning the street earlier, her look searching and concerned. Was she afraid she hadn't lost the two men who'd kidnapped Zack? Or was being cautious the nature of her business?

A dense silence fell over the table even with the clatter of the café around them. Samantha looked uncomfortable. And he knew he was the cause. He'd come on like gangbusters, wanting to date her, romance her, refusing to get out of her car until he had her phone number. Then he'd backed off big-time.

He knew he should say something now. But he couldn't imagine what. *It's been fun,* didn't really cover it. Nor did *Thanks for everything.*

Not half a block down the street, he noticed, there was a sign for car rentals. He could walk to it once they'd finished eating. Wouldn't even have to get back into the Bronco with Samantha and Zack. He felt an almost desperate need to return to his old life as quickly as possible. To touch base with the guiding principles that had gotten him this far. To decide what to do next. Never before had he needed a plan more than he did right now.

Amazingly, Zack put away most of his food in record time. Samantha picked at hers, her attention seeming to wander. Will caught her watching the street again. Or maybe she was just avoiding looking at him.

"Well," he said, when they'd all eaten as much as they were going to. "It looks like I can get a car right up the street—" He motioned toward the car rental sign.

Her gaze followed his and she nodded, then looked at him again as if she felt the need to say something. But the moment seemed to pass. No doubt, she didn't know what to say any more than he did.

"My treat," he said, and reached for his wallet—then stopped.

They both turned to look at Zack. This time Samantha didn't say a word, just held out her hand.

The boy shrugged sheepishly and produced Will's wallet from his backpack. Samantha's look when she handed it to Will told him he was right: she knew she needed to see what else was in there.

Maybe she'd get lucky. It was probably too much to hope that Zack had taken the kidnappers' wallets, but maybe whatever he was protecting would help her keep the boy safe. Will was distrustful of Zack's father and even more so of his "birth" mother. It didn't appear the kid had anyone he could depend on. Except Samantha.

"We'd better get going, then," she said to Zack, and got to her feet.

Will got up, too, and watched Zack slide out, pulling his backpack after him. Whatever it held, it wasn't much. The contents barely made the cloth bulge, even with the CD player inside.

As Will held the door of the café open for Samantha and Zack, he tried not to notice how tiny and defenseless the boy looked. Nor how small his protector was. Or how very female.

They stepped out into the warm sunshine, the cloudless sky overhead wide and clear blue. Anyone watching might have thought they were a family. Will doubted anyone could have guessed the truth.

Samantha stopped just outside the door. ''I'm…sorry,'' she said, and then shrugged, reminding him of the boy. The simple gesture said it all.

''Me, too. It's been—'' *fun, frightening, embarrassing, crazy* ''—interesting,'' he said.

She smiled a little at that. A slight breeze tugged at the golden tendrils around her face. Then she turned and walked toward the Bronco, her hand on Zack's small shoulder. Will watched her push a stray lock away from her face as she fumbled in her pocket for the key to the passenger door.

''Samantha,'' he heard himself call after her.

She turned.

''Good luck,'' he said lamely.

She nodded.

He shifted his gaze to the boy, automatically checking for his own wristwatch and wallet. ''See ya, Just Zack.''

''Bye.'' The boy dipped his head in a way that reminded Will how many times Zack must have had to say goodbye in his young life.

Before he could do anything stupid, he headed for the rental agency, fighting the urge to look back, unconsciously listening for the roar of the Bronco's altered engine.

AS SAMANTHA UNLOCKED the car door, she watched Will Sheridan's long legs walk away. She hadn't expected him to look back. Still she was disappointed when he didn't. Predictable. Just as she'd first thought. But not unimaginative, she amended, remembering his kiss last night.

She opened Zack's door, anxious to get going. Although there hadn't been any sign of the kidnappers, she knew they'd probably be driving something different—just as she was—especially after the Buick's "accident" yesterday.

Zack seemed reluctant to get into the car. She watched him slide the strap of his backpack off one shoulder and glance after Will. "I liked him," the boy said wistfully.

"Yeah, me, too," she grudgingly admitted as she dropped her hand to Zack's dark head. "Come on, let's get moving, okay?"

STILL NO SOUND of the Bronco's engine. Will swore under his breath. What was the point of a souped-up Bronco, anyway, if it couldn't zoom her out of his life as quickly as possible?

He slowed his steps, arguing with himself and losing. "Ah, hell," he groaned as he stopped walking.

As he turned, he heard an engine roar. For a fleeting moment, he thought it was the Bronco's.

From out of a side street, a dark green Oldsmobile came flying around the corner behind the café, and roared into the parking lot, headed for the Bronco.

Time jumped into overdrive. Will saw it all happening too fast. The Olds skidding up beside the Bronco. Samantha and Zack still next to the Bronco's open door, Zack just moments from being safe inside.

Two men. The one Zack had called Al sitting behind the wheel of the Olds. The larger Ralph leaping out to grab Zack. Getting a handful of backpack and T-shirt. Dragging the boy toward the waiting car.

Chapter Six

Will was running before he even realized he was moving. His legs pumped hard, but his movements seemed slow and futile. All he could do was watch as Samantha flew at Ralph.

She kicked out at the kidnapper and wrenched the boy free, the backpack falling to the ground as she tried to get Zack to the safety of the Bronco.

Zack was yelling something Will couldn't understand, fighting her as he strained to reach for his pack.

Ralph snatched up the fallen backpack from the ground, grabbed Samantha's shoulder and spun her around, breaking her grip on Zack. The kidnapper backhanded her. She fell against the Bronco, as the kidnapper lunged again for the boy.

But Will got there first. Already in motion, he hit Ralph full force with a body block. The kidnapper slammed into the side of the Olds with a loud *thunk,* dropping the backpack. Ralph spun and came at him, head down, charging blindly.

Will dodged Ralph's charge, catching the large man in the side with an elbow and a jab to the jaw.

Out of the corner of his eye, he saw Al start to get out of the Olds, as Samantha forced Zack to the open door of the Bronco.

"What the hell's going on?" a coarse male voice boomed from the back of the café.

Al slammed the car door, grinding a few gears as he fought to get the car into reverse. A limping Ralph scrambled around to the passenger side and barely got in before Al tromped on the gas and, gravel flying, sped away. Heading east. The same direction Samantha and Zack would be going.

He stared after the kidnappers, his heart thundering. He couldn't remember a time he'd been more afraid. They'd come after Zack. Again.

"Is everything all right?"

He turned at the sound of the voice. A burly cook stood in the café doorway with a meat cleaver in his beefy hand.

"Fine," he called.

The man nodded, then turned, shaking his head, and went back into the kitchen. Across the narrow street, several people eyed them from the back of a sporting goods store.

Will bent to scoop Zack's backpack from the dirt, still shaken. How many kidnappers tried to grab a little kid in broad daylight? Especially when they knew the second time what they were dealing with: Samantha.

When he straightened, he saw that Samantha had the boy in her arms, crushing him to her, her expression a mixture of fear and anger and relief. She looked up at Will, determination burning in her eyes, revealing a strength of will that might have surpassed his own.

The moment she released Zack, he ran straight for Will, hand outstretched, face pale.

He handed the boy the backpack. Zack hugged it to his thin chest. Tears welled in the large dark eyes. What was in that damn backpack, anyway?

Will shifted his gaze to Samantha. But she wasn't looking at the backpack or the boy's reaction to it. She was staring at Will.

"Are you all right?" Her voice sounded close to tears, and she looked scared. With surprise, he realized her fear now was for him.

He felt a bubble of pleasure, was touched by her concern. "I'm fine," he assured her with a smile. Then he noticed the bruise darkening her cheek where Ralph had hit her. His gut clenched.

"We'd better get going," she said, putting an arm around Zack's shoulders, her gaze coming up to meet Will's. "Thanks."

He shrugged, desperately trying to come up with a good reason why he couldn't go to Seattle. Of course, she wouldn't want him along. She'd feel she had to protect him as well as Zack. But he liked that about her.

"No, I mean it," she said. "Thank you."

"You had it covered," he assured her as he stepped over to the Bronco to open the passenger door for Zack.

She seemed to hesitate before she went around to the driver's side, as if she thought she should say something more.

"Goodbye. Again." She opened her door.

He just nodded and leaned into the car. "Get in the back," he whispered to the kid.

Zack was fast on his feet, both physically and mentally. He grinned, then hopped in the back seat and buckled up, as Will straightened to look over the roof of the Bronco at Samantha.

"What are you doing?" Her tone made it clear she not only knew, but was dead set against it.

"Going to Seattle. Unless I can talk you into taking Zack to the police and letting them handle this."

"I can't do that, Will."

He nodded, not in the least surprised. Hadn't he known there was a lot more to this? Common sense warned him to walk away. Who knew what he was letting himself in for? And he could be pretty sure Samantha wasn't going to tell him. On top of that, he'd lay odds that she still didn't have a plan. That in itself should have sent him packing.

But for the first time in his life, something stronger made him slide into the front seat and close the door behind him. If he'd had to put a name to it, he'd have called it insanity.

SAMANTHA STOOD LOOKING over the roof of the Bronco, breathing deeply as she counted to ten. The man was impossible. He didn't have a clue how dangerous this was or what was at stake. *She* didn't even know. But she knew one thing for sure: nothing was going the way she'd thought it would. The kidnappers had tried to take Zack *again* and in broad daylight. Something was very wrong, and the last thing she needed was some contractor playing hero.

She counted to ten again and then climbed in without looking at him. "Do you have any idea what you're doing?"

"Not a clue."

"This doesn't have anything to do with you."

"Or you, right?" he asked. "It's just a job, right?"

His tone made it clear he suspected this case was personal. "Speaking of jobs, don't you have one you need to get to?" she asked, finally looking over at him.

He smiled, although a little regretfully, she thought. His blue eyes were bright behind his wire rims.

"Actually, I'm on a leave of sorts. Some personal things I needed to tend to. But they can wait."

He was just being a nice guy. And here she'd thought guys like him were extinct. They could be— if she let him get involved in this.

"Please, let me handle this," she said more kindly.

He buckled his seat belt. "Believe me, I won't get in your way. I'm just going along for the ride. I've heard Seattle is nice this time of year."

She shook her head. "I know you want to help—"

"You really don't expect me to walk away knowing those men haven't given up?" he said, his gaze suddenly intent.

So this *was* about protecting her and Zack. Under other circumstances it might have been funny, since she was trained for this and he wasn't. She took a deep breath. He'd gotten in a couple of lucky punches in the café parking lot. But he didn't realize the kind of people she was dealing with. He was a nice man with a comfortable, ordinary life, and he'd mistakenly thought the two of them had that in common.

"Will, I appreciate your worrying about us, but I have to tell you, there's a good chance it's going to get a lot more dangerous, and quite frankly, you aren't—" She waved a hand through the air. He was no Van Damme. "Trained for this."

He raised a brow. "But you are, right?" He smiled at her, all hundred watts.

He did have a wonderful smile.

"I promise to stay out of your way. Just ignore me."

Ignore him? He had to be kidding.

Desperate, she thought about trying to force him out of the car at gunpoint. Great idea. She'd seen this particular set of his jaw before. Well, she could always handcuff him again. But she had a feeling it would take more than a kiss next time.

"Is there anything I can say to change your mind?" she asked with a sigh. "Or make you come to your senses?"

"Not until we reach Seattle and Zack is safe."

He had no idea what that might take. *She* had no idea what that was going to take. She glanced back at Zack. He looked pleased Will was coming along.

She looked at Will again and felt a sharp pang of guilt. She'd done this to this man. Taken a perfectly normal man, kissed him, handcuffed him and ruined him.

If he kept behaving this out of character— She hated to think what he'd do next. She'd have to watch him closely.

Come on, admit it, you like having him along.

Right, just what I need—a man who wants to protect me even though he doesn't have a clue from what.

Exactly.

It's stupid.

You think it's kind of sweet. And you know Zack likes him.

Mumbling under her breath, she started the Bronco and backed out, wondering when she'd be seeing the kidnappers again. At least now she knew it was just a matter of time. The kidnappers wanted Zack too badly. Zack *and* his backpack.

WILL FELT STRANGELY light-headed, senses heightened, heart pounding, adrenaline pumping.

Reckless, was more like it. It was as if someone had taken control of both his mind and body. He was wearing another man's clothing. Riding in a souped-up Bronco. On the run from criminals. With a woman who was all wrong for him and a five-year-old thief.

And amazingly, what surprised him the most was that he couldn't remember the last time he'd felt so good.

He watched for the dark green Oldsmobile as they drove through the sleepy little town of Malta. He didn't think the kidnappers would make another move on them in town. But what did he know?

She pulled up to the stop sign across from Honker's convenience store and gas station at the junction for Highway 2. Then turned west.

"We need another car," she said.

He glanced around. "Do you want me to look for one you can hot-wire?"

She glanced over at him askance. "I don't steal cars—" she said, sounding offended. *Just kids.*

"I have a cousin who lives in Butte. We can borrow his pickup."

"Another cousin?" he asked in disbelief.

"It's a big family."

"I should say. Just how many cousins do you have?"

She shook her head. "On both sides of the family? A lot. I've never bothered to count them."

He couldn't imagine a family that large. His had been small—just his father, mother and sister. His father's work required him to travel a lot, moving his family with him, never settling for long in one spot. If he had a lot of relatives, he wasn't aware of them.

The Bronco cruised down the two-lane, the land flat, pale-yellow dry and smelling of autumn. In the distance he could make out the purple smudge of a mountain range.

She hadn't driven far when she pulled down a fishing access road and stopped beside the Milk River, flushing a flock of Canada geese. The river water was brown, low and slow-moving.

"Zack, sweetie," she said, shutting off the engine to turn in her seat. "I'm sorry but I need to look in your backpack."

Will glanced over his shoulder to see Zack slip off one earphone. "What?"

He was pretty sure the kid had heard her the first time and was just stalling.

"I need to look in your backpack," she repeated. "Please. It's important."

Reluctantly, Zack lifted the pack from beside him, cradling it in his lap for a moment before he slowly handed it to her.

Will watched with anticipation as Samantha dumped the contents onto the console between them. He was immediately surprised by how little was inside. And nothing, unfortunately, looked all that interesting. Just kid stuff. Candy and gum, some worn Pokémon cards, several Hot Wheels cars, a pen, some cash, a half-dozen CDs, several keys on a ring, and what looked like a credit card.

He watched her rummage through the pile, wondering if he'd been wrong about something being hidden in the backpack. He wasn't sure what he'd expected. Something of value. Jewels. A treasure map. Stolen plans. A microchip worth millions. He read too many mysteries.

She picked up the cash, counted out more than fifty dollars, then dropped the bills into the pile again. She sorted through the CDs, fingered the keys for a moment, then looked back at the boy.

Zack sat perfectly still, poleaxed with what appeared to be fear. What was he scared she'd find?

"What are the keys for?" she asked.

"My house," he said, his voice small, barely a whisper. "And stuff."

Will reached back to reassuringly squeeze the boy's thin arm. "What's your house like?"

Zack seemed torn between watching Samantha dig through his backpack and talking to Will.

"It's little," the boy said quietly. "But I have my own bedroom."

Samantha picked up the credit card and studied it. She put it back down. He could see the name on it was Robert Walker. It didn't belong to Al or Ralph, unless those weren't their real names.

"Where did you get the credit card?" she asked Zack.

The kid shrugged. "Ralph."

"And the cash?"

"Ralph."

It was clear Ralph hadn't *given* either to him.

Would Al and Ralph have tried to grab Zack again to get back fifty bucks? Will didn't think so. He watched her sort through the rest of the items, making a stack of the CDs, several of which appeared to be computer games. Alien Attack by the Spider Planet. Weird World Warriors: The Final Battle.

She searched through everything, studying the Pokémon cards as if she expected them to be altered in some way. She even checked inside the empty candy and gum wrappers.

Will picked up the pen. It was from a Seattle bank. He unscrewed it and looked inside, immediately realizing he wouldn't recognize a microchip if he saw one. He screwed the pen back together and handed it to Samantha.

She glanced at it, but didn't appear to find anything of interest, either. He wondered if *she'd* know a microchip if she saw one.

"Zack." She reached back to take his hand. "Those men took a heck of a chance trying to grab you in town like that. They seemed to want your backpack pretty badly.''

The kid said nothing, just looked at her with saucer eyes, unblinking.

''There has to be something they want in it,'' she said. ''Can you think of what it could be?''

He shook his head as if it were a mystery to him, as well.

Will doubted that. Samantha sighed and inspected the pack itself. Nothing hidden in the seams or lining. He studied the measly pile of possessions. Some pilfered. Most worth very little. Even the CDs looked well used. And yet the kid protected that pack as if it held his most prized possessions. Maybe it did.

Samantha put everything but the credit card and cash into the pack again and handed the backpack to the boy. ''I'm sorry I had to look through your things, but I'm worried about you. I have to find out why those men are after us, so I can stop them.''

He nodded and took the pack, set it on the seat beside him and looked down at his lap. After a moment, he pulled his headphones back onto his ears. The music leaked out like faint noise. The kid seemed to zone out again, lost in his own world—a world that had become very dangerous for the little boy.

''His father let him play those violent computer games?'' Will whispered to Samantha.

''His father probably *designed* those games. And I would imagine Zack has been playing them since before he could walk.''

''Could explain his burgeoning talent for crime,''

Will grumbled. A thought struck him. "Could the kidnappers be after one of the games?"

"I thought of that. When we get to a computer, we'd better check them out. I don't know anything about computer games. Do you?"

He shook his head, picking up on the fact she'd said "we'd" better check them out. He'd always thought computer games were a waste of time, but he didn't bother to tell her that. She already thought he was stodgy enough, without his confirming it.

"I have a cousin near Seattle who's into computers. We can show them to him. He might know something." She looked over at him. "What?"

"Sorry, I was just thinking. The kidnappers had Zack *and* the backpack for a good day-and-a-half, right?"

She nodded.

"If there was something in the pack, they'd already have taken it, wouldn't you think?"

"Unless they couldn't find it, either," she offered.

"Or unless they *did* take it, then Sticky Fingers back there swiped it—just like he did Ralph's money and the credit card—*after* Al and Ralph had given him the backpack again. Otherwise, Ralph's money and the credit card wouldn't be in there, right?"

They both turned to look at Zack. He was staring at them, his eyes wide and worried, not even pretending he wasn't listening to their conversation.

ZACK WASN'T TALKING, though. Samantha's attempts to get him to speak were met with monosyllables and shakes of his head. She didn't force the issue, hoping that he'd eventually open up to her. Before it was too late.

She watched him for a moment in her rearview mirror. He'd dug his Hot Wheels out of his pack and now played some demolition derby kind of game on the seat, his headphones still emitting a song she was becoming a little too familiar with.

"Well, it's a great theory, anyway," she said to Will as she turned back to her driving.

He grinned. "See, having me along wasn't such a bad idea, after all."

She shot him a look. Was it possible he could look any more handsome? "I wouldn't go that far. The kidnappers are still out there, and who knows how desperate they'll get."

"Yeah," he said, and looked up the highway, his jaw set, all humor gone from his face.

She felt drawn to him suddenly in a way she couldn't even explain.

She turned her attention to her driving. And her case. It scared her even to think how little she knew about any of this. She'd been running blind from the beginning. She had no hard facts about Lucas's disappearance or the burglary, little knowledge of his and Zack's lives over the past five years, and too many feelings about the people involved.

She'd leaped to the rescue without even stopping to consider the consequences—something she normally never did because it could get her killed. Nor did she know anything at all about the computer game business, if this had anything to do with Lucas's work. It seemed likely, since Whiz Kidz had been broken into about the time of Lucas's disappearance and Zack's kidnapping. But she couldn't be sure of that. Any more than she could be sure that Lucas had set this up as a way to get himself and Zack out of Seattle. There was just too *much* she didn't know.

But she had Zack, she reminded herself. And in a few hours, she'd see Cassie and, she hoped, get some answers. What bothered her, though, was why Cassie was involved at all. After five years of being absent from Lucas's and Zack's lives, Cassie certainly seemed to know a lot about Lucas's personal business and Zack's problem with stealing. Cassie had been the one who'd warned her about Zack's tendency toward theft.

She felt anxious and assured herself that if Cassie didn't give her the answers she needed, there were people in Seattle who might know something. Like Lucas's second ex-wife, Mercedes. Or Lucas's partner in Whiz Kidz.

All she had to do was get there. As she cruised down Highway 2, she wished there were another highway. Unfortunately, this was the only one that ran across the top of the state, stretching a little more than fifty miles south of the Canadian border and almost straight as a stick. The problem was that Highway 2 would also be the kidnappers' choice.

Except, she would be dropping down soon, heading for Butte. Would the kidnappers anticipate that she might make a stop by her office?

She felt boxed in, and knew some of that feeling was due to being confined in the Bronco with Will Sheridan. He seemed to fill whatever space he inhabited with that incredible force field of his. She drove at the new state speed limit, seventy-five, and tried to ignore him as he'd suggested—all the while keeping on the lookout for the green Olds. She didn't think the kidnappers would go to the trouble of changing rental cars, but then again, she'd never thought they'd keep trying to take Zack, either.

"Wanna play a game?" Will asked Zack.

"What kinda game?"

"When I was a boy, we traveled a lot," Will said. "It was before CDs and computer games. So we played road games."

She glanced in the rearview mirror to see Zack mug a face. He probably couldn't imagine a time before computer games.

"Sounds lame," the boy said, but sat up a little straighter, as Will began to spell out the rules.

"This game's for babies," Zack complained when Will had finished. But he looked out the window as if already looking for the items he must find to win. "I see the first barn!" he cried excitedly.

She listened to the two play. Will was great with Zack—even had him laughing. She wondered about Will's own childhood. *We traveled a lot.* After seeing how his sister lived, she could just imagine his childhood, so different from her own. While her parents and siblings vacationed on camping trips to Yellowstone and Glacier parks, Will was probably touring Europe.

Everything about them was so different, she reminded herself.

Maybe that's why they say opposites attract.

Attraction isn't the problem.

So what is the problem?

We're like oil and water, and everyone knows they don't mix.

But oil and vinegar do, and quite nicely.

If you want to make a salad.

"Sam? Sam!" Zack called from the back seat. "You have to play, too."

She smiled back at him. "You're too good for me."

The boy began to explain the rules to her. She joined in, soon remembering she used to play games like this with her family. It made her feel almost nostalgic about her large extended family and the summers spent camping with aunts, uncles and cousins galore.

After a while, the sun filled the Bronco with warmth, the game ended and Zack fell asleep. She liked Will's easy way with Zack. He must be a natural, she thought, knowing from her research that he had no nieces or nephews or any children of his own.

He seemed relaxed, as if this were nothing more than a road trip. Maybe for him it was. She wondered why he'd come along. Was it only because he felt she and Zack needed protecting? Or was it possible—

"Want to tell me about it?" he asked, startling her from her thoughts.

"About what?" She felt her cheeks flush.

"You and Lucas."

Startled, she sucked in air and avoided his gaze. Was she that transparent? Or was Will that perceptive?

"Here's the way I figure it," he continued as she struggled for words. "You believe Lucas staged the so-called kidnapping just to get himself and Zack out of Seattle and away from whomever is supposedly after him. Lucas then planned to pick up Zack at Grandma's rest home. He got Cassie into the plan to get you to Wolf Point. How am I doing so far? Am I close?''

Dead-on. She could feel his gaze on her. ''He might have been desperate enough if the police were looking for him and he couldn't chance picking up Zack himself.'' She sounded defensive, even to her own ears.

''Wouldn't the kidnappers have told Zack that they were taking him to his father?''

She'd thought of that. ''Maybe they did. Maybe that's why Zack is acting so protective.''

Will was silent for a moment. ''If that were true, then wouldn't Zack be upset with you for keeping him from his father?''

Good point. Zack had almost acted as if he'd expected her.

''Also, if you believed that Zack really hadn't been kidnapped, then why intervene? Why not just let Lucas pick up Zack at Grandma's? After all, Lucas is wanted for questioning by the police. Why get involved?''

Got you there, doesn't he?

''But Lucas *didn't* show,'' she countered. ''Even after two days.''

He said nothing, as if waiting for her to dig herself in deeper.

''On top of that, Cassie hired me to make sure Zack was safe. And anyway, this is what I do for a living.'' She felt defensive as hell and not sure why.

She didn't have to explain herself to this man. Who'd asked him along? If he thought he knew so much—

"Are you still in love with Lucas?"

The question came out of nowhere and hit her like a baseball bat. She gulped air as she swung her head around to look at him again.

His denim-blue eyes were somber behind his glasses. He waited as if he really expected her to answer.

She opened her mouth, a denial already on her lips. How did she feel about Lucas? Not the way she used to, that was for sure. "It's a long story."

He nodded and leaned back as if to say he had plenty of free time right now.

She chewed at the inside of her cheek, surprised that part of her actually wanted to tell him about it. Needed to tell him. Or at least someone. The only other person who knew the whole story was her cousin Charley, and that was because they'd been going to college at the same time. Everyone else just knew that she and Lucas had broken up. That she'd had a car wreck. But that she wasn't hurt badly. Not even Lucas knew *everything*.

How much did she want to tell Will, a man she'd never laid eyes on until a few days ago?

She glanced over at him. Her heart did a little flutter-step at the compassion she saw in his expression. Her eyes stung. It was as if he already knew. Well, at least some of it.

"You don't have to tell me if it's too painful," he said quickly, looking apologetic.

She shook her head. "I want to tell you." She desperately wanted to tell someone, and as Will had pointed out, they had the time. Also, she knew she wouldn't be seeing Will Sheridan again after they got to Seattle.

She blinked away the tears and bit the bullet. "Lucas and I met in college." Concentrating on the road ahead, she waded in slowly. "We dated."

"I see."

She feared he did see. That he saw a lot more than she wanted him to.

"Cassie was my roommate. I introduced her to Lucas. She was dating a different guy every night in those days." Not that it mattered. She took a breath. This was harder than she'd thought it would be. "Lucas and I had a disagreement one night over when we should get married."

"It had gone that far?" Will said.

She nodded. "Lucas wanted to wait until he had a job and could give me the kind of life he thought his wife should have. He was ambitious and worried that a wife would hold him back. I just wanted us to be together." Had she really been that naive that she thought love could conquer all?

"We argued. Lucas left. Cassie went after him to talk some sense into him, she said." She took a breath. "Lucas was upset and had been drinking when she found him. Cassie had a few drinks with him and they talked and—" She sneaked a look at Will.

He had an I-think-I-know-where-this-is-headed look on his face.

She nodded and sighed. "They ended up sleeping together, although Lucas swore he couldn't remember any of it. Cassie got pregnant. Lucas was overcome with guilt. He did the honorable thing. He married her. End of story.''

She waited for him to be sympathetic, to say the things people always say. *Sorry. How awful for you. It probably wouldn't have worked out, anyway.*

''You really loved him.''

''Yes,'' she said, surprised how quickly she could admit it to Will. But she suspected he'd somehow already guessed the truth.

''Your first love?''

Her only love so far. She nodded.

''But they divorced.''

''Yes, right after Zack was born. After the dust settled, Cassie didn't want Zack any more than she did Lucas.'' She cringed at the bitterness in her voice.

''But you still did. Still do.''

Her gaze flicked over to his. She swallowed. Did she still want Lucas? And Zack? ''I— I—'' Isn't that why she'd hardly dated over the past five years? Hadn't she just been waiting for Lucas to come back to her and bring Zack, the son *she* should have had with him?

''I understand now why you took the case.''

She thought of Lucas's call on the night of the party. It hadn't been a message to meet him in Wolf Point. He'd only said he was in trouble, needed her help, needed her to look after— Something for him. Zack? No message of undying love. No remorse. No call begging her to forgive him.

You could have grown old waiting for that *call.*

He loved me. I know he did.

Was taking the case really about Lucas? Or about

what happened the night she learned of Cassie's pregnancy and Lucas's upcoming marriage to the wrong woman—the car wreck and the debt she felt she now owed?

She pushed away the painful memories. It was definitely too complicated to explain to Will. She didn't even understand it herself.

''I did it because of Zack,'' she said simply, hearing a ring of truth in that, and was grateful when Will dropped the subject.

He settled back in his seat and turned his gaze on the passing scenery. Zack, still asleep, had his cheek pressed to his backpack. She drove, lost in the past, slowing only for the small towns they passed through as the sun traveled with them west and storm clouds gathered on the horizon.

Just outside Great Falls, the first flakes of snow sifted down from a pewter-gray sky.

''I'm hungry!'' came a cry from the back seat.

Big surprise. ''We'll stop at the town just ahead,'' she told him. But no more cafés. Luckily, Zack would be happy with burgers and fries and another shake. And Will— Well, he'd asked for this.

With the Bronco smelling of burgers and fries, she left Great Falls with Will digging into the bag o' burgers. She hadn't seen a dark green Olds. Hadn't seen much traffic at all—not unusual for this time of year. Most of the tourists had all packed up and left, and it was a little early for hunters.

They filled themselves with food, washing it down with a gallon of cola. Then Will got Zack involved in another game, and Sam put some miles behind them.

The flat open land gave way to rocky bluffs, mountains and ponderosa forests, as the day bled into afternoon and the shadows grew long and dark, the light snow continuing to fall.

She couldn't wait to see Cassie, and yet she also couldn't shake a sense of foreboding. Or the feeling that Cassie knew something important about Lucas's disappearance and that it wasn't good.

But it was more than that. Cassie was that link with the past and Lucas. And that link brought back a lot of suffering.

It began to snow hard at Wolf Creek, icy flakes blowing sideways across the highway. Visibility dropped to a few yards in front of the car, and she had to slow to a crawl.

It continued to snow all the way into the "Mining City." It was after eight when she finally pulled into the parking lot at the Butte mall and saw the clock over the main entrance. The mall would be closing in less than twenty-five minutes. She just hoped Cassie had waited.

She glanced over at Will. "What is it?" she asked, when she saw the worried expression on his face.

"Look, you're obviously better at this than I am and you know the people involved. It's just that—" He shook his head, frowning.

"No, what were you going to say?"

He rubbed his stubbled jaw with the flat of his palm for a moment. "It just seems to me that this disappearance and kidnapping might be a ploy."

"A ploy?" She felt her heart rate pick up as she

looked past him, through the falling snow to the nearly deserted mall.

"I probably read too many murder mysteries, but it feels like you've been lured here. I'm just worried that you might be walking into a trap."

Chapter Seven

Will couldn't put his finger on what had him so anxious. Maybe the fact that Samantha would be a fool to trust someone like Cassie. Look what had happened the last time she'd trusted the woman. Or Lucas.

But he knew it was more than that. There was something Samantha wasn't telling him. He could sense it—something deep and dark and painful. And he would just bet money it had to do with Lucas.

He watched her stare out through the snowfall at the mall. The dated building was a long nondescript rectangular one. The lights illuminated the falling snowflakes and the few snow-covered cars still in the lot, ghostlike under the cloak of darkness and snow.

"I appreciate your concern," Samantha said as she shut off the Bronco. "It's one of the reasons I agreed to meet here at the mall. It's public. And I have a plan."

She actually had a plan! That perked him up a little.

It was obvious she still had feelings for Lucas. It shouldn't have bothered Will. Shouldn't have given him a pang of jealousy. Or made him dislike the guy all the more. Shouldn't have—but did.

"I have to meet someone in the food court."

She glanced at him and seemed to wait for him to say something. Was she wondering how much he'd overheard on the phone this morning? Obviously she didn't want to talk about Cassie in front of the boy.

"I thought we could all go in, and you and Zack could window-shop. That way I'll be able to see you from the food court," she said.

He liked the idea of being able to keep an eye on her, as well. "You got it." He turned to Zack for his okay. The boy was sitting up staring at the building through the snowy darkness, looking worried. "Hey, kid, I'll bet Samantha will bring us a couple of corn dogs when she's done."

Zack seemed to brighten a little. "With mustard and ketchup?"

"Sure, and don't worry, Will is going to be with you, and I won't let either of you out of my sight."

Will carried Zack across the deserted lot to the mall entrance through air thick with snowflakes, Samantha pensive beside him.

"When was the last time you saw her?" he asked quietly.

She glanced over at him but didn't ask whom he meant, no doubt realizing now that he'd overheard her phone conversation.

"Almost six years. Not since she told me about her…wedding plans."

No wonder Samantha seemed a little nervous.

He wondered if she had a gun in her purse. As much as he disliked the idea of her with a loaded weapon, he hoped she did. He just wanted her safe. Whatever it took.

Once inside, he and Zack wandered toward the other end of the mall, while Samantha walked toward the smell of tacos and egg rolls and cinnamon buns and popcorn.

But Will didn't go far. He had no intention of letting Samantha or Zack out of his sight. "Let's stop here for a moment," he told the boy.

The food court was small, only a half-dozen tables surrounded by a bunch of orange plastic chairs halfway down the mall. A couple sat at one of the tables, eating and talking. A woman with her two rowdy young children sat at another. He could hear the woman trying to get the kids to stop fighting and eat.

A man sat alone at another table, sipping from a plastic cup. He seemed to watch Samantha approach, but Will knew that didn't mean anything. Any red-blooded male would have to be blind not to notice a woman like her.

"I used to have one of those—" Zack said. The boy was pointing at a bike in the store window.

"Where is it now?"

Zack shrugged. "It was red. I think I outgrew it. Dad was going to get me a bike. But we had to wait."

For a moment, Will thought the boy might go on. But it was obvious he felt he'd said enough. Wait for what? Will wondered. Had Lucas really been planning to skip the country? Was Samantha right about Lucas setting up Zack's abduction? Then why hadn't Lucas shown up in Wolf Point?

"Well, I think it's high time you had another

bike,'' Will heard himself say. "Once we get to Se-attle—''

"Really?" Zack's eyes glittered with excitement. "A big one like that one?"

"Absolutely." What was he doing making promises like that? By tomorrow the boy might be taken away by the authorities, and Will might never see him again. The thought bothered him a lot more than he wanted it to. "Of course, we'll have to find a place for you to ride it."

Zack ducked his head. "It's okay if I don't get it," he said, as if he'd been promised things before and had already learned promises often weren't kept.

"Hey," Will said, squatting in front of the boy and taking the thin shoulders in his hands. He waited for Zack's gaze to meet his and saw the tears. "You *will* get one of those bikes. You have my word on it. And I don't give my word lightly. You believe me?"

Zack studied him for a moment, then nodded slowly.

Will smiled. "Good. You just let me know what color."

The boy grinned, eyes bright. "Red. It has to be red."

Glancing down the mall, he saw Samantha go over to the taco joint and order something. He wondered what she was going to say about the bike. He hoped she didn't see it as interfering. He'd done enough of that.

She turned with a cup in her hands and moved to one of the tables to sit facing them. She looked a hell of a lot more relaxed than he felt right now.

Only a few stragglers wandered the mall, still shopping. He wondered what Cassie looked like, and thought how hard it must be for Samantha to see her again after all these years.

He disliked Cassie even without having met her. She'd abandoned her own child. And she'd hurt Sam and Zack. As he and Zack moved along the fronts of the stores, he swore he wouldn't let Cassie—or Lucas, for that matter—get the chance to hurt Samantha or Zack again. Even if it meant staying a little longer in Seattle than he'd originally planned. As if anything he'd planned hadn't gone completely awry since the moment he'd laid eyes on Samantha.

SAM SIPPED the strong bitter coffee and studied the shoppers, watching for Cassie. The woman had been slim and blond in college. But for all Sam knew, Cassie could have changed her look entirely. In fact, she suspected her former roommate might be one of those women who was always impulsively dying her hair the hottest new wild color and changing her hairstyle to suit her latest mood.

So she kept Will and Zack in view as she searched the faces of the shoppers for a petite woman with a greedy look. Her own unflattering description of Cassie surprised her. Is that how she'd always felt about her? But the description fit. Cassie had come from money and lots of it. One of the first things she'd told Sam was that she had no intention of losing that money. All she had to do to keep getting her monthly checks from Daddy was to not get kicked out of school.

When Cassie had gotten pregnant, she'd been

afraid her father would disinherit her. Maybe that's why she hadn't noticed how devastated Samantha had been. She hadn't seemed to care that she'd just stolen Sam's happiness and a whole lot more.

But while Cassie's father had thrown a fit, he'd given his blessing, because, fortunately, Lucas came from a family with a good enough pedigree. He had probably been glad to let some other man take care of Cassie.

So what had Cassie been doing since the divorce? Maybe more importantly, what was she doing back in Lucas's and Zack's lives?

The large grandfather-style clock near the mall entrance gonged a few minutes before nine. Shopkeepers began to drag the barred doors closed, and a quiet uneasiness settled over the building.

She glanced up at Zack and Will. They were standing in front of a sporting goods shop down the mall and seemed to be talking intently about something in the window. Will's easy way with Zack never ceased to amaze her. She smiled to herself and shook her head. She wasn't surprised how fond Zack seemed to be of the man.

As she looked around, she saw that only a few shoppers were left, and those seemed to be heading for the exits. Even the woman a few tables away finally gave up trying to get her children to finish their fast-food meals. She chased after the children, toward the snowy darkness outside.

Either Cassie had been here earlier and left, or she'd never shown at all. It made Sam all the more anxious. Why had Cassie agreed to meet her and then not waited? She couldn't shake the memory of Will's comment that she might be walking into a trap.

She pulled out her cell phone and tried her office again, reminded of what Cassie had said about going to the office if they missed each other at the mall. The line was still busy. That was odd. Even if Cassie had gone there and caught Sam's associate Andrew Berg still around, that didn't explain the line being busy for almost ten minutes now.

Before the food court closed, she bought two corn dogs with packets of ketchup and mustard to go. Then she walked down to meet Zack and Will.

The mall was officially closed, the shop doors barred, the cleaners beginning the task of getting the place ready for the next day. But still no Cassie.

"I take it she didn't show," Will said, sounding relieved.

"No. I need to stop by my office for a few minutes." She turned her attention to Zack. "Did you find anything you wanted?"

He shook his head and shot a look at Will as if they shared some secret. "Did you get us a corn dog?" he asked, noticing the paper sack in her hand.

"Would I forget my two favorite men?" she joked, instantly regretting her choice of words. Don't get too used to having Will around, she warned herself. He's just signed on as far as Seattle, and he might come to his senses long before then.

In the Bronco, Zack wolfed down his corn dog and eyed Will's, still in the sack. She doubted Will was a corn-dog fan, and wondered if he had been saving it for the boy.

"I'll flip you for it," Will said, seeing the boy's

interest. He pulled a quarter from his pocket. "Heads or tails?"

Zack thought for a moment. "Heads."

Will flipped the coin, caught it in his hand and looked down at it, then at Zack. She could clearly see it was tails. "It's heads," he said, and handed a delighted Zack the other corn dog.

She smiled over at Will, suddenly very glad she'd kissed him at the party and started the chain reaction that had him here with her tonight.

Just think what could happen if you kissed him again like that.

Perish the thought!

Right.

Just the thought of Will's lips on hers sent a shudder through her.

"Cold?" He reached over to turn up the heater.

"Thanks," she said as she pulled out of the parking lot. But she didn't dare look at him for fear he'd see from her flushed cheeks to the heat at her center.

MURPHY INVESTIGATIONS was in an old brick building that had been a fancy hotel in its time. It now looked out on the defunct open-pit mine with its gaping hole more than one mile wide and its inky bottom filled with water.

Her building stood alone among the ghosts of other structures, only their crumbling foundations still remaining. The area had an abandoned feel to it, just as a lot of Butte's old downtown area now did. Empty buildings stood on what had once been one of the richest hillsides in the world, next to what had been the largest city in Montana.

But Butte, with its tough-guy persona, had always been home to Sam. It seemed to fit her like a pair of old jeans. It might not be pretty, but it was comfortable.

She'd chosen her office location because of its privacy and cheap rent. Also, she didn't like the modern office complexes down the mountainside. Her office opened out onto one of the original hotel balconies. For safety reasons, a stairway had been built down from the balcony as a fire escape. Probably a good idea, considering the condition of the building.

As she parked in front, she saw that Andrew's car wasn't on the street. In fact, there were no other cars on the narrow street, as far as she could see.

"Nice view," Will said, looking at the lights of Butte through the snowfall.

The mountain glowed with the lights from the original city, which trailed down the hillside, puddling in the valley where the "new" Butte had been sprouting up for years. Where the mall was.

She glanced back at Zack. He'd fallen asleep again. It was way past his bedtime, and all the driving had worn him out.

"I just need to run in for a minute," she said to Will. He nodded. The message passed between them without words. He'd watch Zack and lock the doors behind her. "If you need me—"

She knew she didn't need to finish.

Will nodded. "I'll honk. Don't worry, we'll be fine."

"I won't be long," she promised. She left the Bronco running with the lights out but heater and wipers on. Still, she didn't like leaving Will and Zack alone. Especially on a lonely street in the middle of a snowstorm with kidnappers still on the loose.

The massive oak door of the building was locked, just as it should have been, which made her feel a little better. She used her key to get in—but stopped the moment she turned on the overhead light and stepped inside. There were wet tracks on the worn hardwood floor, as if someone had just been here. Or was still here.

She advanced slowly, listening intently for any sound. The four-story building felt as empty as the mall had been just minutes before. But then, it was past nine. She walked down the hallway under the golden haze of the bare bulb, the old wood floor creaking under her step.

Her office sat at the back of the building on the second floor. She pushed open the stairwell door, feeling the cold dense air rush around her. The wet tracks led up the stairs. She climbed to the second level and cautiously pushed open the door, noticing immediately that the tracks headed in the direction of her office. She slowed, reassured by the weight of the pistol against her ribs, but concerned by a sound she couldn't place.

She stopped, her pulse pounding, as she looked toward her office. It took her a moment to realize what she was hearing. And why she could hear it at all. Her office door was open. And the phone was off the hook, the awful steady beeping sound echoing down the hallway.

She pulled the .357 from her shoulder holster and moved cautiously toward the open office door. As she reached it, she peered inside.

The outer office had been ransacked just the way her house had been days earlier. As she stepped in, she picked up the phone from the floor with her gloved hand and put it back on the hook.

The beeping stopped. Silence filled the office, as heavy as concrete.

As she glanced into the adjoining room, she saw that it, too, had been ransacked. The desk light was on, casting a warm glow over the worn top of her oak desk.

Carefully she began to step through the debris to her office, then stopped when something caught her attention. A splatter of dark brown spots on the wall. More on the pale wood of the floor. She swallowed, her heart hammering as she moved closer, her weapon ready.

She spotted the shoe sole first, and for one horrible moment she thought it might be that of her associate, Andrew Berg. But in the glow from the desk lamp, she saw that the man sprawled dead on the floor behind her desk was much too short and thick to be Andrew.

She turned away to squeeze her eyes closed, fighting back the small cry of mixed surprise and fear and revulsion. She wasn't one of those women who got queasy at the sight of blood. But she knew she'd never get used to seeing violent death. Murder shook the foundation of her belief system, making her question if man really was inherently good. It was one of the reasons she'd become a private investigator and not a cop. She didn't often stumble across dead bodies in her line of work, and she liked it that way.

Right now, she wished she'd taken her Aunt

Edie's advice and become a dental assistant. Looking into people's mouths couldn't be any worse than this.

She opened her eyes. Al, the short, "nice" kidnapper, had taken a couple of bullets up close and personal in the chest. He lay sprawled on the floor, his eyes open but sightless, two very distinct holes in the left breast pocket of his gold-colored down coat. He was dead. Very dead.

Suddenly her heart took off at a trot. She noticed something odd. Tiny gosling feathers were stuck to the bloody coat and other feathers stirred restlessly as if there was a breeze in the room.

Her eye caught a movement. She jerked the .357 up, her finger just a hairbreadth above the trigger. The ancient drapes over the window that opened to the balcony billowed out. Someone was behind the curtain! Her trigger finger cramped in those seconds before her mind processed what she was seeing. The window was open; it was only the breeze blowing the drapes.

Relieved, she stepped past Al to close the window, but as she came around the end of the desk, she saw something that froze her.

Her heart pounded fiercely in her chest as she followed the line of the dead man's arm. Using her sleeve to avoid leaving fingerprints, she carefully picked up the lamp and shone the light on the crude letters scrawled in dark brown blood on the side of the desk.

The man Zack called Al had died writing the letters *CA*, the *A* trailing down to a squiggly line just above Al's hand.

An icy finger of fear ran up her spine. Ca—Cassie?

Is that what he'd been trying to write? She felt cold soul-deep at the thought—

The sound was faint but distinct. The soft creak of a floorboard. In that instant, she realized she wasn't alone.

She spun around, leading with the weapon, trailing with the lamp, but she wasn't fast enough. Hands savagely twisted the gun from her hand and knocked the lamp away. It hit the wall, the bulb shattering in a burst of light.

She got only a glimpse of her attacker before she felt the blow to her temple. She went down hard, landing on her side. Something cold pressed against her cheek, a wet spot on the rug where the snow had blown in from the open window. Pain radiated through her head. She tried to get up. But before she could move, she felt a needle plunge deep into her thigh. She let out a weak cry just before her mouth was covered with thick tape.

The drug was fast-acting, but not so fast that she didn't feel the heavy mildewed fabric of the huge bag as her body was stuffed into it and the drawstring pulled tight.

Chapter Eight

Through the falling snow, Will stared at the office entry where he'd seen Samantha disappear minutes ago. The wipers click-clacked back and forth, as hypnotizing as the snow but a lot louder.

"Are you warm enough?" he asked Zack.

No answer. He looked over his shoulder to see Zack still sound asleep in the back seat.

Carefully, he reached over and shut off the engine, turned off the wipers. The night closed in. The snow fell in a silent cloak, making him feel all the more isolated. The lights of Butte seemed dimmed and distant.

He glanced at his watch, a little surprised he still had it. Did this mean he was gaining Zack's trust? The thought pleased him. He studied the time. Samantha had been gone for over five minutes. He just wished she'd come back out. The last thing he wanted to do was sit out here in the dark, thinking stuff he shouldn't be thinking—and worrying about her.

But he couldn't seem to help himself. He didn't like the idea of her going in there alone, but he reminded himself it was her office building and this was her job. And he was only along for the ride.

Right.

He considered the classic brick building with its gingerbread trim. They didn't build them like this anymore. Too expensive. It was a shame, though. The brickwork was beautiful.

The diversion didn't work. He couldn't get his mind off Samantha. If things had gone the way he'd planned, he and Samantha would have been sitting in a nice restaurant right now, talking over wine and a delicious dinner. Instead, he was sitting in a dark car that smelled like greasy burgers, baby-sitting a kid she'd stolen. And she was—

What *was* she doing? He glanced at his watch, growing more anxious by the minute. A light flashed on, then off quickly, in the alley behind the building. It took him a moment to distinguish its source, to make out the shape: the back half of a dark-colored van. The vehicle must have been parked there the whole time. He just hadn't seen it through the snow and darkness, and wouldn't have if the driver hadn't opened a door and caused the inside dome light to come on.

His heart hammered in his chest. Where was Sam? He stared at the van through the snow, suddenly very worried.

Damn. He didn't like this. Not at all. He hesitated, not wanting to leave Zack—even for a minute. It was probably nothing. He waited, torn between taking care of Zack and checking on Samantha.

Minutes ticked past. The van hadn't moved. He couldn't be sure if the driver was still inside. He rolled down his window to listen. The snow silenced the night.

He spotted movement by the van and heard a low curse. He could make out two dark figures now, as they came around the back of the van. They both wore coats with the hoods drawn up. One was slighter in build than the other. They were carrying something.

His heart began to pound. It appeared to be a large stuffed laundry bag.

It was the shape of the full bag that set his mind scrambling: the contents resembled a body. The two figures had the bag between them, each holding one end. It appeared to be heavy, as they trudged slowly through the snow.

He reached over and pulled the keys from the ignition, flipped the dome light so it wouldn't come on, then eased open his door, locked it and slipped out.

With the Bronco door locked and Zack asleep inside, he could buy a little time. But he desperately needed a weapon. He moved down the side of the building toward the van. He stopped at the corner. He could hear hurried voices at the side of the van.

"Pick up your end, dammit," the man snapped irritably.

"I'm doing the best I can," whined a female voice. "It's heavy."

Instinctively, Will reached down, and from a pile of rubble worked an old brick out of the snow. It wasn't much of a weapon, but beggars couldn't be choosers. He moved quickly, refusing to think about what was in the bag. *Who* might be in the bag. He let out a yell and raised the brick as he came out of the darkness at the edge of the building, hoping a surprise attack would have the effect he needed.

The woman dropped her end of the bag and ran for the van door. The man seemed to hesitate, just as Will had feared, and reached into his coat with one hand while still holding on to the end of the bag with the other.

Will was on him too quickly for him to do much more than release the bag. It thumped to the soft snow. Will brought the brick down hard. The brick did little more than glance off the man's shoulder, but the forward motion and the blow drove the man back against the side of the van.

Suddenly something gleamed in the man's hand. *A gun.*

The sound of the van engine turning over ripped through the snowy stillness. For one heart-stopping moment, the man seemed torn between giving up whatever was in the bag, and leaving with the van and the woman driving it.

But then the van lurched and the man scrambled after it, barely able to jerk open the passenger door and get in before the vehicle roared away down the alley and disappeared into the night.

Will dropped to his knees in the snow, his heart slamming against his ribs at what he saw sticking out of the top of the bag. A lock of golden-brown hair.

Frantically, he fought to untie the drawstring. It gave, and he opened the bag, hurriedly uncovering Samantha's face. Jerking the tape from her mouth, he felt for a pulse.

His relief made him weak. Sam's pulse was strong and steady.

As the sound of the van's engine died off in the distance, he pulled the bag from her body, scooped her up from the snow, and carried her to the Bronco. When he neared it, he saw that Zack was awake and looking out the window, his eyes huge.

"What's wrong with her?" the boy cried.

"She's all right," Will said as he slid Sam into the front seat. Zack climbed up to sit beside her.

She murmured something in her sleep, a groggy, almost drunken sound. That and her apparent lack of visible injury lead him to believe she'd probably been drugged. Something mild enough that she was already starting to come out of it.

"She's just sleeping," he assured Zack.

The boy looked skeptical. He was no dummy.

Will climbed behind the wheel, not sure where to take her. Someplace warm and dry, for starters. He would prefer to take her to the hospital, but he knew he'd be risking a possible brush with the authorities. The last thing he wanted to do was get Samantha in trouble with the law. Like she wasn't already. And considering the alternatives, he felt Zack was safer with Sam and him than with anyone else right now. At least, until they could find his father and get to the bottom of all this.

He reminded himself that he was now neck deep in it. That should have shocked him. Scared the hell out of him. At the very least, worried him. What had he gotten himself involved in? Had he lost his mind?

"She's going to be okay," he said, wondering whom he was trying to reassure—Zack or himself.

He squeezed the kid's narrow shoulder, then reached over to smooth Samantha's hair back from her face, the bruise on her cheek from earlier now dark against her suntanned skin. She sighed in her sleep, and he felt a terrible weight on his heart that he feared would never go away.

He found a motel on the edge of Butte where he could hide the Bronco from view of the highway, then carried Samantha into the room, Zack in their wake. She was starting to come out of it. In the distance he could hear sirens.

He put her down on the bed and began to take off her boots. Zack stood guard over her, a determined look on the kid's face. Once Will got her coat and boots off, he covered her with a blanket, trying not to think about her in that bag. Or the two people who had drugged her and put her there. He hadn't gotten a good look at either the man or the woman because of the hooded coats they wore and the snow. Just an impression of evil.

Samantha mumbled softly, her eyelids flickering. He got up and went to get a cold washcloth. When he came back, Zack was sitting next to her, holding her hand. The scene squeezed his heart like a fist.

"Here, put this on her forehead," he said, handing the washcloth to the boy.

Zack did as he was told, then sat studying Samantha's face.

"We probably should just let her sleep for a while," Will told the kid. He glanced toward the second bedroom. "I think there's a TV in there. I'll holler when she wakes up."

Zack seemed reluctant to leave Sam, but finally

agreed. A few moments later, Will heard the sound of the TV.

He turned his attention back to Samantha, only to find her looking up at him, her eyes wide and pupils dilated.

SHE SAT UP too fast. Everything started to spin, and she fell back, closing her eyes against a wave of nausea. "Where am I?"

"In a motel room."

"Zack—" Her eyes flew open as she tried to get up again.

Will gently pushed her back down. "Zack is fine. He's in the other room watching TV." He sat down on the side of the bed. "He'll be glad to see that you're awake."

She focused on Will as she tried to still the nausea. Her head hurt and she felt sick. But still, he was the best-looking thing she could ever remember seeing. "What happened?"

"You don't remember?" he asked softly.

Something dark at the edge of her memory shoved its way in. *Oh, God.* She closed her eyes again as everything came back in nauseating waves of fear and revulsion. Al's body behind her desk. Someone at the window. The blow to her head. The prick of a needle in her thigh. And the bag. Oh, God, the smell and feel of the rough fabric of the bag covering her face—

Her eyelids snapped open again. She tried to sit up; something cold and damp slid over her face. A washcloth. She caught it before it fell to her lap, vaguely registering that Will had gotten a cloth for her.

"I found Al in my office. He'd been shot twice in the chest. And then I heard something at the window—"

He took the wet cloth from her and pressed it to her cheek.

She covered his hand with her own and closed her eyes. "I heard someone behind me—" she could feel the lump on the side of her head throbbing "—someone hit me and drugged me." She opened her eyes, the horror too real. "The bag. They put me in a bag."

"Forget about it," he said gently. "It's all over now. You're safe. Zack is safe."

"But how—" She spotted Will's coat over by the door, still dripping with melted snow, his boots soaked as well. She looked up at him. Water droplets still clung to his hair.

He'd come after her. He'd saved her.

Tears welled in her eyes, emotions rushing over each other. Gratitude that he hadn't listened to her and come after her when he had. Fear that something could have happened to him and Zack. And disappointment in herself. She'd needed him—and she didn't *want* to need him.

"Did you see who did it?" she asked, trying to pull herself together.

"A man and a woman. That's all I can tell you. I didn't get a good look at either of them. It was dark and snowing so hard. They were bundled up. She was slight in build. The man was medium height, medium build. Sorry I can't give you more."

The descriptions could fit anyone. Except, she distinctly remembered seeing a flash of blond hair just before she was hit. *Cassie.* And the man Sam had heard in the background on the phone? *Lucas?* The thought rattled her. She forced it away as she pulled the washcloth from her cheek and balled it in her hands to still the shaking.

"You're all right now," he said. His fingers glided like a breath over her cheek. He brushed a lock of her hair back from her face, his gaze kind and caring, and almost her undoing.

She sat up a little, leaning back against the pillows he'd plumped behind her head. She sucked in deep breaths, trying desperately to corral her emotions.

"They were going to kill me," she whispered, the fear so real she could still smell the bag over her head, the tape covering her mouth.

He took the washcloth from her and put it on the nightstand. "If they wanted to kill you, they'd have shot you like they did the kidnapper. I don't think they wanted to kill you. I'd say the bag was probably meant for Al."

She shivered. Maybe the bag *had* been for Al. Because if it had been for her, they would have known beforehand that she would stop by her office. And the only way they could know that was if they knew she was supposed to meet Cassie tonight.

Cassie could have been the woman whom Will had described and whose name Al had tried to write in his blood. *CA—* What more evidence did she need? But the man— Not Lucas. She couldn't believe he'd burglarized the company he worked for. Let alone that he was involved in— Murder.

She closed her eyes. They'd put her in a bag. They'd had some plan for her. Dear God.

"I should call the police," she said, knowing that was true. A man had been murdered in her office.

"I don't think that's a good idea."

She opened her eyes, unable to believe Will Sheridan had said that.

He shook his head and smiled a little at her shocked expression. "You were right originally to protect Zack by not going to the authorities. Someone wants that boy, and until you find out what's going on, I think he is safest with us."

Us. She loved the sound of that word falling from his lips.

"Samantha?" Zack asked tentatively from the doorway between the two rooms.

She smiled and held out her hand to him. He seemed to hesitate, but only a moment. He came to her, and she drew him into her arms, hugging him tightly.

"I'm all right," she said, realizing it was true.

"I was going to order a pizza," Will said.

Zack lifted his head from her embrace. "Pizza?" His eyes lit up.

"That's a great idea." She knew he was just trying to keep things normal for Zack. She licked her dry lips, her face sensitive where the tape had been. Here with Will and Zack, things did almost feel all right. Temporarily. She didn't kid herself that it would last.

"Get the phone book and find us a pizza joint," he said to Zack. "How about a hot bath?" he suggested to her, as the boy went into the other room to look for the phone book. "Might make you feel better."

"Yes."

He insisted on carrying her into the bathroom. She rested her head against his strong shoulder, relaxing in the warm, safe feel of his arms around her, listening to the steady, sure beat of his heart and breathing in the male scent of him.

She felt intoxicated as he set her down while he drew her water. Her inebriation had nothing to do with being drugged.

"I can manage now, thank you," she said, when he'd filled the tub. "Thank you," she said again, this time for a lot more than the bath, knowing there weren't words to thank him enough for saving her life. She looked into his blue eyes, bright behind his glasses. "Are you sure, Will?" she whispered, so close to him she could barely catch her breath. "Now that we know just how dangerous it is."

He took off his glasses to wipe the steam from them with his shirttail. "My heart is set on seeing Seattle."

She nodded, feeling tears of gratitude rush to her eyes. "You must think I'm not much of a private investigator," she said, biting her cheek as she watched his face.

He shook his head and smiled. "You're the most amazing woman I've ever met. You were just outnumbered. In a fair fight, I'd put my money on you anytime, Sam."

Sam? He'd called her Sam. Her heart leapt foolishly in her chest. No one had ever made those three letters sound so intimate.

He cupped her face with his hand. The strong, capable hand of a man who worked for his living. Maybe they had more in common than she'd first thought. She touched his hand.

"You sure you'll be all right in here by yourself?" Will asked her, his blue eyes dark with obvious desire. "I could wash your back."

She swallowed, consumed with the thought of the two of them in the tub. The temptation was almost too much.

"I thought we were going to order a pizza," Zack said from the doorway behind them. He held the phone book in his hands.

"I assume you've already decided what kind you want," Will said.

"Pepperoni-and-sausage with extra cheese," Zack said still waiting in the doorway.

"You'd better see to Zack." She smiled.

He nodded and smiled back at her. "Maybe another time," he whispered. "Just holler if you need me."

Oh, she'd needed him, all right. But she hadn't hollered. He'd just been there, saved her, and she'd probably never know exactly how he'd done it. She didn't want to need him. Couldn't. When the time came and he was no longer around— She didn't want to think about that now.

All she knew was that she'd underestimated this man.

Just as she'd underestimated just how dangerous this case was. She wouldn't make either mistake again.

Chapter Nine

By the time she came out of her bath, she felt a little better, though still shaken, still confused. But more determined than ever to keep Zack safe and find out what was going on.

And yet she couldn't shake the memory of the kidnapper lying in his own blood, having tried desperately to leave a message. Where was Cassie? And Lucas? They both seemed to be missing now.

This case had gone from what she thought was a simple abduction by a parent to…murder. Every instinct told her to turn this over to the authorities. Legally, she was required to come forward. She could lose her P.I. license, maybe even go to jail, if she didn't. But she also couldn't take the chance that the authorities would give temporary custody to Zack's birth mother. There was no hard evidence against Cassie. Yet.

Because of that, Samantha couldn't be sure that Cassie wouldn't avoid arrest and somehow get her hands on Zack.

But she couldn't forget the glimpse of blond hair she'd seen just before someone had hit her, drugged her and stuffed her into that bag. She hugged herself, chilled to her soul by the memory. Cassie was slightly built, blond, and had said she would stop by Sam's office if she missed Sam at the mall. And hadn't Sam known as well as anyone what Cassie was capable of?

But *murder?*

"Do you want some pizza?" Zack asked, looking at her with concern as she came out of the bathroom.

She smiled to reassure him and went over to see what kind of pizza they'd ordered. Loaded. She took a slice to be polite and prove that she was fine. Even Zack didn't eat with his usual enthusiasm. He appeared worried about her, and her assurances didn't seem to help.

"Can I watch TV in my room?" he asked, leaving some pizza uneaten.

"Sure," Will said, and ruffled the boy's hair as he passed.

Zack tossed a smile at him over his shoulder as he went into the other room, jumped on the bed a few times, then settled down to watch whatever was on the tube.

"You're good with him," she commented.

Will laughed. "Believe me, I'm just winging it. I know nothing about kids."

"But you've always wanted some of your own."

Subtle, real subtle.

He looked away. "Oh, yeah. Someday."

A heavy silence fell between them. She wondered what she'd said wrong. "Well, you're a natural. You should have a half-dozen."

He began to clean up the pizza mess. She watched

him, wondering about his sudden evasiveness. There was so much to wonder about Will. He'd saved her life. But she felt a lot more than gratitude. Not good. Will wasn't the kind of man who'd ever let himself fall for a P.I.

And that's what she was, wasn't she? She reached for her purse and dug out her cell phone. When the dispatcher at the police department answered, she asked for her father.

"Where are you?" he demanded, obviously trying to keep his voice down.

She heard him shut his office door.

"I've been worried sick about you," he said in a more normal voice.

"Why, what's happened?" she asked innocently.

"A man was murdered tonight in your office."

Someone had called the police. "You're kidding."

"Where are you, Sam?" her father asked again.

"On my way to Seattle. Is Andy—"

"He's fine. He wasn't there at the time, fortunately, and he says he doesn't know anything."

"Who called it in?" she asked, ignoring her father's skepticism.

"Anonymous caller."

Big surprise. "Any idea who the dead man is?"

"Al Knutson, better known as Al the Ox, a former professional wrestler turned small-time crook. I assume you didn't know him?"

"No."

"He's from the Seattle area. But we didn't find any vehicle around your office. Pretty odd, since no one in his right mind would walk around in that neighborhood at night. Sam?"

She braced herself. "Yes, Dad?"

"You're sure you don't know anything about this?"

"It's a mystery to me," she said truthfully. She hated not being more honest with him, but she couldn't put him in a position where he'd have to keep anything from his chief, and she wasn't going to turn Zack over to the cops. Not yet. Especially now that she feared Cassie was involved.

"But I'll keep in touch, Dad. I should be back in a few days." What were a few days, anyway? Then she'd tell him everything. He wouldn't be happy about it, but soon she'd have some answers. At least, more than she did now. "I'm sure Andy can handle anything that comes up."

She hung up and looked at Will. He was waiting expectantly. "Someone called the cops. They know about Al." She took a breath. "Can you drive?"

"Seattle?"

She nodded. "It's the last place Lucas was seen."

And Lucas was the key to this mess. "But first we need a different vehicle. We'll borrow my cousin Tommy's pickup."

THEY WERE OUTSIDE Missoula, the wind howling, snow turning to rain and splattering on the windshield, when her cell phone rang.

She shot a look at Will. He frowned. Almost afraid, she answered it before it could ring again and wake up Zack.

"Hello?"

Silence. "Sam? Oh, thank God, you're all right,"

Cassie cried. "I was so scared when I saw the police cars and heard there had been a murder."

Samantha looked at Will and mouthed *Cassie.* "I missed you at the mall," she said into the phone, unable to keep the accusation from her voice.

"I was there at eight," Cassie said quickly. "When you didn't show up by eight-fifteen, I got scared and left. Is Zack all right?"

"He's fine. Where are you now?" she asked tersely.

"You don't think I had anything to do with what happened at your office?" Cassie sounded flabbergasted by even the notion.

"You admitted you were there tonight."

"No—I mean, yes, I went *by* there."

"Alone?" Sam asked.

"What are you getting at?"

"I went to my office because you said you'd check there if you missed me at the mall. I found a man dead behind my desk." She didn't mention the letters Al had written in his own blood. "Someone attacked me. The attackers were a man and a woman. A woman with blond hair."

"It wasn't me." Cassie sounded scared.

"Why do you suddenly want to see Zack so badly?" Sam demanded, checking first to make sure the boy was still sound asleep between her and Will.

"I told you. I need to see my son."

"I don't believe you. I think you'd better level with me, or I'm going to go to the police with what I do know, which is that you were at my office tonight."

"I told you—"

"It doesn't matter what you told me," Sam snapped. "Maybe the police can get the truth out of you."

Silence. For a moment, she thought Cassie might have hung up.

"I'm scared, Sam." All the bravado was gone from Cassie's voice. "I'm afraid someone is after me."

"After you?" Sam said, not buying this. "Why would someone be after *you?*"

"Because of what Lucas did."

Sam's heart thudded. "I'm listening," she said, and glanced over at Will. In the faint dash light, he looked worried.

"Lucas called me a few weeks ago. He said he'd done something stupid. He owed some people money and had promised them his latest project. But he said he couldn't go through with it. He sounded desperate. He said he was working on something big—so big that he thought they might try to kill him for it."

Outside the pickup, large wet drops of rain smacked the windshield, spiraling out of the darkness like comets. "You have to be kidding."

"No. He told me he'd taken precautions to protect his design."

"What kind of precautions?"

Again Sam thought she heard hesitation in Cassie's voice. "He planned to divide the game into pieces."

"And do what with them?"

"Hide them, I guess, until he was free of the men who were after him," Cassie said. "I thought he was just being paranoid. Then Zack was kidnapped—and

I got one of the pieces of the game in the mail. And a note.''

Sam caught her breath, her heart pounding. "A note?''

"It says, *'In case something should happen to me, and you receive this package, take the CD to the police and tell them it is one of five pieces. They will understand why the game is so important once they put the pieces together. For your own safety, do not keep this piece of the game.'*''

Sam swore under her breath. If it wasn't for Zack's kidnapping, she'd think this was just a publicity stunt for the new game.

"Don't you see, Sam, if this game is as big as Lucas said it was, then anyone who gets a copy is in danger.''

"Not if you turn it over to the police as Lucas instructed,'' Sam pointed out.

Silence.

Sam took a breath and held it, a terrible feeling pushing against her chest with the force of an elephant. "That is what you did with it, right?'' she asked.

"No,'' Cassie said in a small voice. "I can't. I heard from the men who have Lucas. They are demanding all the pieces of the game. Or they will kill him.''

"Kill him over a *computer game?*'' Sam cried in disbelief.

"Obviously you don't know anything about the computer game business,'' Cassie said. "If this game is as big as Lucas thought it was, then it could be worth millions.''

Millions for a game? She guessed she *didn't* know anything about computer games. But Cassie sure seemed to know a lot about not only computer games but Lucas, a man she'd dumped five years before.

Sam closed her eyes, her head aching. She didn't know what to believe. Why would Lucas send a piece of the game to his first ex-wife? And how would the men who had Lucas even know about Cassie?

"I think these men were behind Zack's kidnapping," Cassie was saying. "I think they planned to use Zack to get the game pieces but now that you have Zack—"

That bad feeling had settled deep in her chest and refused to budge. "Who else did Lucas send pieces of the game to?" Sam interrupted.

"That's just it," Cassie said, "I don't know."

Sam thought of her ransacked house. Was it possible the person who broke into her home had been looking for a piece of the game? But she'd already checked with Andy. No letters or packages had come from Lucas.

"This message," Sam asked, "the one from the men who have Lucas, do you still have it?"

"Yes," Cassie said. "It is type-written and arrived in the same mail as the CD and Lucas's note."

It was raining hard now, water pinging off the hood and cab.

"You have to find those other pieces of the game," Cassie pleaded. "To save Lucas."

To save Lucas? Suddenly, Sam saw things a lot clearer. "You knew I'd drop everything to come to Zack's rescue. And you made it so easy for me, predicting that Zack had been taken to the rest home in Wolf Point. That was a nice touch, letting me think that Lucas might have staged the kidnapping, that he might be planning to pick up Zack there. And I played right into your hands."

"No," Cassie protested. "You're wrong, I—"

"You used me," Sam interrupted. "And now you think you can use the way I once felt about Lucas to force me to find the pieces of the game for you."

"It's true," Cassie said quietly. "I called you because I knew you were the one person who would care enough to find my son. And, yes, to save Lucas."

Sam tried to contain her anger, at Cassie, at herself. She *had* dropped everything just as Cassie knew she would.

"You still don't believe me, do you?" Cassie said, sounding hurt. "Don't you see that I was just trying to protect my son and his father?"

"Why the interest now, after all these years?"

Chilly animosity filled the line. "I love my son, no matter what you think."

"Right. You know, I thought I knew what you were capable of after what happened in college with Lucas. You proved back then that you would do anything to get what you wanted. Just like you got Lucas. But this time we're talking murder. They still hang killers in Montana. And you think I'm going to let you use me again?"

Will had been right. This was a trap. Just not the kind of trap he'd feared. She looked over at him, her emotions close to the edge now.

All the anger she'd kept bottled up all these years

at Cassie poured out like the rain streaming down on them from the darkness overhead.

"It *was* you tonight at my office, Cassie. What had you planned to do with me? Not kill me like you did Al—because you still need me, right? Where's Ralph? Or is he who you're working with?"

"Sam, you have to believe me. It wasn't me. It was whoever has Lucas. If you don't help him—"

"You expect me to *believe* you?" Sam demanded. "Especially after what happened tonight? Did I mention that the kidnapper left the name of his killer in blood?" She waited for Cassie's reaction, but heard nothing on the other end of the line. "He wrote the letters '*CA,*' *CA* as in Cassie."

She finally got a reaction.

Cassie let out a startled cry. "Not Cassie. Catastrophe. He was writing the name of Lucas's game."

Lightning splintered the sky in front of the pickup, a jagged edge of blinding white. The line went dead. Sam stared at the phone in her hands for a moment, then clicked off, her hand trembling, her heart a sledge inside her chest.

"You were right," she said to Will. "I did walk into a trap." She told him about her telephone conversation and Cassie's claim that she'd received a note from the men holding Lucas. "She was betting that I would help Zack and Lucas." Cassie knew her so well. That was the problem with once-best friends. They could use that knowledge against you and become your worse enemy.

Will didn't seem all that surprised. "What are you going to do now?"

"Try to find Lucas," she said without hesitation. "He is the missing piece."

"You're afraid Cassie might be telling the truth," Will said.

Cassie tell the truth? It seemed inconceivable. And yet, if she was—

"Yeah," Sam said after a moment. "I guess I am."

Will swore and shook his head, his gaze taking in the sleeping little boy between them. "All this over a stupid computer game?"

Sam watched the night rush by for a moment, unable to shake the feeling that there was a lot more at stake than a computer game.

WILL DROVE through the night. The rain followed him all the way to Seattle, an unrelenting downpour that made the highway slick and the night seem darker and colder.

But he knew the chill inside him had nothing to do with the weather. His suspicions had been true. The kidnapping had been a ploy to get Samantha involved. And it had worked. He felt scared. For Zack. For Samantha. Her former roommate had used Sam's love for Lucas against her. Just as she had years ago. Now Zack and Samantha were pawns in some game.

He felt overwhelmed with anger and a rush of protectiveness. If Zack or Samantha were hurt because of this...

But he knew it was too late. They had already been hurt.

He looked down at the boy. Sam kept Zack snuggled asleep against her, her arm around him. She held on to the boy as if her love alone could keep him safe.

And she did love Zack. That was plain to see. But did she still love the boy's father, as well? Will was just thankful that he'd come on this trip to Seattle with her, he thought protectively. She and Zack needed him.

He concentrated on his driving, feeling a lot more than protective of the woman. Sam hadn't said much since the phone call. He figured she was probably still in shock after what had happened to her. What had happened to Al. It definitely had Will stunned and scared. Then Cassie's revelation about Lucas. And the kidnapping. Samantha's head must be spinning. He knew his was.

Someone had upped the ante from kidnapping to murder. Any thoughts Will had of heading home when they reached Seattle went out the window. He was sticking this out. Just to make sure Samantha and Zack were safe. To make sure Samantha didn't do anything stupid. Like get mixed up with Lucas O'Brien any more than she already had. Or Cassie. Had the woman holding the other end of the laundry bag with Sam inside been Cassie?

He had a sick feeling he'd be seeing the duo again, and not under the best of circumstances. Only now, he suspected that the murderer wanted more than Zack and his backpack. He feared the killer wanted Sam, as well. According to Sam, Cassie hadn't been the only one to call her for help. Lucas himself had left a message.

Will was now part of it. The realization should

have upset him more than it did. He had no idea what he was doing, just that he was doing it and it felt right. He was determined not to examine things too closely.

As he listened to the steady clack of wipers and swish of tires splashing through the rain-puddled highway, he thought about the little boy sitting between them and where this had all begun. How far back did it go? College? What bothered him was this relationship between Samantha, Lucas and Cassie. And now Zack. Sam had been hurt badly before, but he feared this time, now that she'd gotten to know Zack, she was primed for heartbreak. Not to mention what effect Lucas was going to have on her, whether he was dead or alive.

He glanced over at Sam, afraid for her. In the dim glow of the dash lights, the rain streaking the window behind her, he saw her gazing out at the darkness with an intensity that worried him. He was sure she was still scared. A brush with death did that to you—made you realize just how fickle life was. But if anything, she seemed more determined, stronger in some way.

He didn't want to be drawn to that. Any more than he wanted to be drawn to her. It was one thing to want to protect her and Zack. It was a whole other thing to feel this woman's strengths; to be attracted to her sheer determination and her need for justice. Strong stuff, justice. Getting close to Samantha Murphy was more dangerous than he ever could have imagined. Even if she had fit his blueprint for a wife, she still had feelings for another man and that man's child. How much more wrong for him could Sam be?

He chuckled silently to himself, half amazed that faced with all that wonderful logic he still wanted to stop the pickup and take her in his arms and kiss her until the sun came up.

The early morning darkness felt suffocating, the rain unending, all of his senses alert and honed in on the woman sitting across the seat from him. He drove into Seattle—hardly any traffic out this early—waiting for Sam to tell him where to go next.

SAM LOOKED OUT the window as the sleeping city passed by in a wet, dark gray blur. Seattle. She cracked her window and let a blast of cold air in, then rolled it back up. Tired. And yet wired. Still disbelieving. She'd been able to think of nothing but getting here and getting to the truth before whoever was after Zack made another move.

Well, she was in Seattle. And so was Will. For her, it was only the beginning. For him, it was the end of the line.

"Now that you've seen Seattle—"

"I'm staying until I know you and Zack are safe," he said, cutting her off.

"That could take a while."

"I have a while."

She nodded, filled with a surge of joy that made her heart pound harder. Somehow it was easier facing all of this knowing that he was here with her.

Take it easy, girl. He'll be leaving once this is over.

Yeah, but he's here now. And I'm glad. So there.

She took a breath and let it out slowly. "Then we need to catch the ferry to Vashon Island," she told him. "I think it's time we took a look at those computer games in Zack's backpack and I know just the place."

"Your cousin, the computer geek?" he asked.

"That's the one. But most people just call him Charley the Cop."

Will shot her a look of surprise. "I'm finally going to get to meet one of these many cousins—and he turns out to be a cop?"

She smiled. "Yeah, and with a little luck he won't arrest us both."

THE RAIN STOPPED but the clouds still hung over the water, the lights of the city filtering through the gray. A breeze kicked up whitecaps on the water as the ferry pulled away from the dock and headed toward Vashon Island.

Zack woke up wide-eyed to realize they were on a boat. "Can we get out?" he asked excitedly.

Will looked over at Samantha. "All right if I take him up on deck?"

The ferry was nearly empty this time of the morning, and the ride would be short. "I need to stretch my legs, too," she said. "I'll meet you both up front."

Zack beamed. It was good to see him enthused. He'd actually pulled the headphones off his ears; they hung around his neck, that music he listened to constantly finally silent.

Watch him, she mouthed to Will, who nodded knowingly. She wasn't afraid that anyone would try to kidnap him here. She was sure no one had followed them from Montana. But she didn't want any pickpocketing incidents that would call attention to them.

Up on the deck, Sam left them to find the rest room and the snackbar. Now that Zack was awake, he would be hungry.

The ferry carved through the low-hanging clouds, mist swirling around the deck as the sky lightened to the east. Sam trailed along the outside of the boat, hands deep in her pockets, braced by the cold air and the breeze. In the distance, she could make out lights flickering through the fog. There was something comforting about the steady chug of the large engines driving the ferry and the sound of the waves lapping against the side of the boat.

Now that she was in Seattle, maybe she could get the answers she so desperately needed. She hadn't given up hope that Lucas would turn up. She didn't want to believe that Cassie might be telling the truth.

Inside, she found the rest room, freshened up, and bought doughnuts for Zack and two cups of coffee. As she carefully carried the tray through the door to the deck again, she felt the ferry slow and saw that they had almost reached the island.

She started to make her way toward the front of the ferry. Something made her halt. A familiar movement. Or stance. Across the deck through the passenger cabin windows, she spotted a man. He stood on the other side of the ferry, just barely visible through the mist, his collar up on his coat, his hat pulled low to the cold. He appeared to be staring down into the swirling water.

Her heart leaped. *Oh, my God. Lucas!*

Chapter Ten

Without even realizing, she dropped the cardboard tray, the coffee spilling onto the already wet deck.

The front of the ferry disappeared into a cloud of fog. She could hear the motors reversing, the boat slowing. They had reached the island. He would be disembarking in a matter of minutes.

Rather than work her way around the deck, she rushed back inside the passenger cabin and wended her way toward the other side of the ferry and the lone man she'd seen standing at the railing.

Lucas was alive. Zack's father was alive. And she'd been right about Cassie.

She pushed open the door. The fog bank was dense and wet. She shivered as she pulled her coat around her and moved cautiously down the deck toward where she'd seen Lucas. The ferry ground to a noisy stop. The wind poked holes in the fog, giving her only teasing glimpses of the deck.

Working her way along the edge of the railing, her mind raced with questions. Why hadn't he called her? Where had he been? Why hadn't he come looking for his son? But Lucas was alive. Wasn't that all that mattered?

Wisps of fog brushed her face like cobwebs. The ferry ramp dropped loudly to the shore. Engines started on the car deck below as the first vehicles disembarked.

The fog shifted in the wind, opening to expose the deck and the shore.

The man was gone. In that same instant, though, she heard footfalls echoing from the stairwell. She raced to the stairs and practically threw herself down the steps.

She burst through the door onto the lower deck. There he was! Just ahead of her.

"Lucas!" She ran now, weaving her way through the straggle of passengers embarking. "Lucas!"

She reached out, getting a handful of his raincoat sleeve. She tugged.

He came around in surprise, stopping abruptly. She crashed into him, thrown off balance by her forward momentum.

"Excuse me?" he said, looking both annoyed and concerned.

She stumbled back. The man wasn't Lucas. Not even close. But he was wearing the same type of coat, the collar up. She'd followed the wrong man! She glanced around frantically, certain the man she'd seen on the boat had been Lucas.

The man pulled his coat sleeve free of her grasp.

"Sorry, I thought you were someone else," she stammered, stepping back as the man stalked off.

She searched among the departing passengers. There weren't many. None of them resembled Lucas.

"Samantha?"

She turned at the sound of Will's voice and the throb of the Bronco's engine. He looked concerned as he pulled up next to her and reached across to open her door.

She climbed in, suddenly weak and tired and scared. Was she losing her mind? Had she only imagined she saw Lucas? Yet, wasn't that better than the alternative—that he was alive and didn't want to be found? Or that he was being held for ransom?

"Are you all right?" Will asked, frowning over at her.

She nodded and closed her eyes, haunted by the image of Lucas standing at the ferry railing.

CHARLEY MURPHY LIVED on Point Beals in a large beach house with his wife and three children.

"Sam!" Charley said when he opened the door.

Behind him, she could hear the kids and Katie in the kitchen. The smell of pancakes, bacon and coffee wafted through the house.

"Sorry to stop by so early," she managed to get out before Charley pulled her into his arms in a bear hug. He was a big handsome man with dark hair, big brown eyes and more than his share of Murphy charm.

"Get in here," he growled. "Charley," he said, extending a hand to Will.

"This is Will Sheridan and Zack O'Brien."

Charley lifted a brow at the last name as he ushered them all into the kitchen.

Katie looked up from the stove, pancake turner in hand. She was dark-haired, pretty and petite. A perfect match for Charley. They'd met at college, had fallen in love literally at first sight and had been together ever since.

"Looks like we have a few more for breakfast," Charley announced good-naturedly.

Sam gave Katie a hug and said hello to the kids: Reese, four; and Alex and Suzanna, the twins, three. Katie was pregnant again and looked as if she might be due any day.

"I need to talk to you," Sam whispered to Charley.

He nodded. "After breakfast." He drew up more chairs and grabbed place settings for all of them.

They talked about everything but what she was really doing in Seattle. Sam could tell that Will liked Charley and his boisterous family. When they'd finished, Charley led her and Will down the hall to his den. Katie and the kids took Zack to the rec room to check out their toys.

Zack looked back at Sam, his CD player in his small hands, the earphones around his neck. He wore his backpack, but the computer games were now in Sam's purse. Zack had relinquished them with his usual reluctance just before they reached Charley's. She caught a glimpse of the boy's worried expression before he turned into tough-guy again and disappeared with the other kids.

"You realize you should turn the boy over to the authorities," Charley said, sounding like the cop he was the moment they were in the study with the door closed. He was obviously familiar with the case, and knew her history with Lucas and a whole lot more.

"I just need some time to figure it all out," she said. "The kid's in trouble. Maybe Lucas, too."

Charley shook his head at her. "I hate to see you going back down this road again, you know?"

She knew. She glanced over at Will, wondering what he was thinking of all this, wondering how much he'd figured out about her and Lucas. A lot. But not everything. Only she and Charley knew everything.

"I have to try, for Zack's sake," she said determinedly.

Charley nodded and gave her a look that said he knew her well enough to have guessed she wouldn't want to give up.

"I desperately need some answers. What can you tell me about Lucas? Cassie said he was in financial trouble." She told him what had happened in Wolf Point and in Butte, and about thinking she'd seen Lucas on the ferry. Then she detailed what Cassie had told her.

Charley swore, something he rarely did. "I don't believe it. What kind of woman is Cassie? Never mind, don't answer that. I already know." He looked from Sam to Will and back to her.

"Will can hear anything you have to say," she said, reading his concern. "He's...with me."

Both Will and Charley lifted a brow but said nothing about that.

"Lucas was into online trading," Charley said in his cop tone. "In over his head. Word on the street was that he owed the wrong people a lot of money and that he'd made some promises he couldn't keep."

"This computer game he was working on?" she asked.

Charley nodded. "That's what I'm thinking. That he'd promised them the game, if it really is worth anything, and he tried to renege."

"Would Lucas jeopardize his own son like that?" Will asked.

Charley shot a look at Sam, his expression making it clear that he wouldn't put anything past Lucas.

Sam shrugged. She'd thought she'd known Lucas five years ago—and obviously hadn't. She didn't pretend to know him now.

She glanced over at Will. He seemed to be studying the floor.

"I have to be honest with you, Sam," Charley said. "I think Lucas has skipped town with some woman and left you with his mess. Isn't that what he did the last time?"

Will's head came up.

She avoided his questioning gaze. "What if the game is just what Lucas said it was, and someone really is threatening to kill him for it?"

Charley gave her his you're-a-chump look. "Then Lucas is in danger *and* anyone else who gets involved. Drop the case. One person has already been murdered. And you know what extremes Cassie will go to to get what she wants."

She didn't want to talk about Cassie or the past. Nor could she drop the case. "What is Lucas's partner saying was stolen from Whiz Kidz?"

"Bradley Guess? Just the one game—the new one Lucas was working on," Charley said. "It's called

Catastrophe. That's about all I know. Interesting name under the circumstances, wouldn't you say?''

"Catastrophe?" she echoed. Could that really have been what Al was trying to write in blood before he died?

"I'd love to see that game," Charley was saying. He must have caught her look. His gaze narrowed. "Don't tell me *you* have a piece of it?"

"Maybe." She opened her purse and pulled out the games. She handed them to Charley.

He studied the boxes, then the CDs inside. "Maybe he hid the game in another one." He shrugged and swung around to insert one into the CD-ROM. A few seconds later, a game came up on the screen in a flash of color and sound.

"This isn't it," he said, exiting after a few minutes. He put in the other one. "Nope. I've heard of both of these. They've been on the market for a while."

Charley shook his head as he handed her the games, and she placed them back in the boxes.

"I don't like anything about this, Samantha. These game people—" He waved a hand through the air. "Look, I think you're making a mistake, cousin, if you don't let us cops handle this one." He shrugged. "Nor can you keep the kid—"

She started to argue, but he held up his hand.

"I can buy you twenty-four hours and that's pushing it. Twenty-four hours and I turn the boy over to the authorities. In the meantime, he stays here. He's safer here than with you right now."

She couldn't argue that.

"Deal?"

''Deal,'' she said, and gave her cousin a hug. ''Thanks.''

She looked over at Will. He nodded and smiled as if saying that between the two of them they could wrap this up in twenty-four hours. She felt a rush of tenderness for him. He really was part of a dying breed. Twenty-four hours, though, and he'd be gone.

THE MORE WILL FOUND OUT about Lucas and the computer game, the more troubled he felt for Sam. Dynamite couldn't have lodged him from her side. Twenty-four hours and Zack would be turned over to the authorities and possibly to his birth mother— a woman the boy didn't even know, a woman whom Will suspected might be anything but what the boy needed.

Zack needed someone loving and caring and protective and— He needed someone like Samantha Murphy. The thought bothered Will as they said goodbye to Zack.

The boy seemed fine with staying at the beach house with the other kids, as long as he had his backpack, CD and his computer games back.

''We'll see you in a few hours,'' Samantha told him.

Zack shrugged as if he didn't care, but Will could tell that he was pretty infatuated with Samantha. Understandably so.

Samantha was getting attached to Zack, too. Will could tell she had a hard time letting the boy out of her arms. The moment she released him, he scampered down the hall after the other kids, looking a little embarrassed.

Will hated to leave Charley's. He knew Sam and Zack were safe there. He also liked the feel of the large Murphy family and the warmth they seemed to share. How many more cousins were there who would have a vehicle waiting for Samantha should she need one? Or a safe place to stay?

He liked Charley, too, and agreed with him that Samantha was in over her head on this case. But Will had come to know her well enough to realize she wasn't backing down. Not now. Not with Zack in danger.

That was why he was sticking by her side. "What now?" he asked, as they drove away in yet another borrowed pickup.

"I don't know," she said, sounding down.

She had to be exhausted from lack of sleep. He knew he was, and probably wasn't thinking clearly.

"If Lucas was lying about the game," she said thoughtfully, "he might have been just stalling for time so he and Zack could skip the country. But what about the break-in at Whiz Kidz if the game wasn't worth anything?"

"The burglar might not have known that," Will suggested. "Or Lucas could have burglarized his own office to make it look like someone was after the game and him."

She nodded, but he could tell she didn't like thinking of Lucas in this new light.

As they drove back up island the short distance to the ferry, he felt anxious, and knew it was from leaving Zack and worrying about Samantha. Not that he didn't think the kid would be safe with the cop and his family. He just didn't like Zack out of his sight right now, and hurriedly warned himself about getting too attached to either Zack or Samantha. But part of him knew it was already too late. When it came time to leave them— He hated to think about that. *Twenty-four hours.* A lot could happen in that amount of time.

"Are you all right?" he asked Samantha as he drove the pickup onto the ferry. He watched her look around as if she expected to see someone.

"I just keep thinking about seeing Lucas earlier on the boat," she said, her voice soft, almost scared. "I could swear—" She looked up at him. "Or maybe I just wanted to see him."

"Maybe," he offered, wanting to reassure her but not sure what she needed. Lucas could be alive and hiding out from his creditors. He could have staged all of this to make his escape, setting up Samantha to take care of Zack. Would Lucas do that to Zack? Hadn't Zack said something about waiting to get a bike? Maybe this was part of some plan Lucas and Zack had together, and that was why Zack seemed pretty calm about everything that was happening to him.

He watched her hug herself as if chilled by a cold he couldn't feel.

"Maybe I did just imagine him."

Will felt a sharp pain. It took him a moment to recognize it as jealousy. Plain and simple. Damn Lucas, wherever he was.

It was still early in the morning, the day gray and wet, a weak sun trying to battle its way through the clouds. But the traffic on the ferry and in the city had increased.

"I thought we'd start with Whiz Kidz and Lucas's partner, Bradley Guess," Samantha said as the ferry docked again in Seattle.

Will could tell it was hard on her, too, having left Zack. Worse believing Lucas might have been the man she saw this morning, a man more concerned for his own safety than that of his son.

"What can I do to help?"

She smiled over at him. "I was hoping you'd search Lucas's office while I keep Guess busy." She handed him the keys from Zack's backpack. "Unless I'm mistaken, one of these should fit."

THE OFFICE OF Whiz Kidz was located in downtown Seattle, just a few blocks from Pike's Market and the ferry. As Will parked the pickup, Sam stared at the crowd in the market, expecting to see Lucas's face among the passersby. Half afraid she wouldn't. Half afraid she would.

A group was crossing at the light, but she didn't see anyone she recognized.

"You sure you're all right?" Will asked, studying her.

"Sure." She shot him what she hoped was a reassuring smile.

He reached across the seat before she could open her door and squeezed her hand. He looked as if he wanted to say something, but changed his mind.

The sign inside the doorway of the older brick building indicated Whiz Kidz was on the fifth floor. She and Will stepped into the small, antiquated elevator.

"Not exactly cutting edge," Will commented.

Her thought exactly. She was glad when the door opened on the fifth floor and she could get out of the musty-smelling confined space.

She realized immediately that this top floor space was smaller than the floors below. There were only a few offices and there was no reception area, which surprised her.

A short hallway with threadbare carpet ended in an office door with gold lettering on opaque glass that read, Whiz Kidz.

This was where Lucas had designed a computer game worth millions of dollars?

She could see several other offices. Small and simply furnished, they each had a computer, desk and chair. One of the offices had an outer office and a window. The walls were faded as if large poster-size objects had recently been taken down.

There didn't seem to be anyone around. Either computer game whizzes didn't come in early, or there weren't many employees at Whiz Kidz.

A phone rang in the office at the end of the short hall behind another door with gold lettering: Bradley Guess. She headed for the door, eavesdropping on what she could hear of Mr. Guess's one-sided conversation.

There was no door with Lucas's name on it that she could see.

"I'm handling it," the voice snapped irritably. "Look, if I knew something, you'd be the first— Whatever. I don't have time for this now, Bebe." He hung up and swore.

Sam tapped lightly on the glass.

"Come in!" the brusque voice snapped.

She glanced at Will, then pushed open the door. This office was a little nicer than the others, but not much. A large computer dominated the space; next to it stood a stack of computer games. On the walls were several dozen large colorful framed posters of computer game covers. None she'd ever heard of. Which meant nothing.

"Mr. Gu—" She never got the name out. Sitting behind the desk was a man she recognized, but not as Bradley Guess. "Buzz?" she stammered in surprise.

It took him a little longer. He blinked several times and frowned.

"Samantha Murphy," she provided. "We went to college—"

"Samantha, sure. You and Lucas— Yeah, I remember you."

He didn't offer her a seat. In fact, he didn't seem all that excited to see her. Not that they'd been close in college, even though he'd been Lucas's closest friend.

"I didn't know the two of you were partners in Whiz Kidz," she said. Who was she kidding? She didn't know much of anything about Lucas's life.

Buzz nodded, and she tried to remember the name he'd used at college. Not that it mattered. Obviously, he'd changed his name—and his appearance. He looked more "hip" in his button-down shirt, khakis. But he was still short with wiry brown hair and intense dark eyes that always made him look as if he were thinking hard about something.

"So, what are you doing here?" he asked, and shot a look at Will.

Socially he was the same, Sam realized. Inept.

He was staring at them as if they were lost and he didn't like giving directions.

"I'm a private investigator," she said. "I've been hired to investigate the disappearance of Lucas O'Brien." It wasn't entirely a lie. "This is an associate of mine, Will Sheridan."

He glanced at Will again. "I'm afraid I won't be much help. I have no idea where Lucas is."

"When was the last time you saw him?" she asked. "Do you mind if I sit down?"

"I'll wait for you down the hall," Will said, excusing himself as per their plan. He closed the door behind him.

She drew up one of the chairs across the desk from Buzz—*Arnold Zingler*. That had been his name. But everyone called him Buzz because of his buzz cut.

As she sat down, she pulled a notebook and a pen from her purse. "The last time you saw him?" she asked again, flipping open the notebook.

He glanced toward his door as if worried about where Will had gone.

"Well, I've already told the police everything I know," he said. "Why don't you talk to them?"

"I will, but there are a few things I'm not clear on. When did you say you last saw Lucas?"

Buzz sighed, picked up a No. 2 pencil from his desk and leaned back in the chair. He began to twirl the pencil between his fingers like a baton. "I saw him Friday morning when he came in. He seemed agitated, acting weirder than usual." He continued in a singsong voice as if he'd told this story numerous times. "Later that night someone broke into his office. Tore it up, stole his most recent game and destroyed the computers. That's all I know. I haven't seen Lucas since.''

She could tell there was a whole lot more Buzz wasn't saying. He acted nervous, twirling the pencil at Mach-two speed.

''You have no idea why he was acting strangely?''

Buzz shrugged. ''You know Lucas.''

She'd thought so. ''I heard he was in some sort of trouble. Financial trouble.''

Buzz seemed to squirm in his seat. ''Who told you that?''

''Does it matter?'' she asked.

''I wouldn't know anything about Lucas's personal life,'' he said.

It was an obvious lie. She tried a different approach. ''This new game he was working on—what kind of game was it?''

Buzz twirled his pencil and shrugged. ''I really can't say. This is a very competitive market.''

''Really? I'm surprised you don't have more security, then.'' As far as she could tell, they didn't have any.

''It's never been a problem before Friday night.''

''How did the burglar get in?'' she asked.

''Broke in through a service entrance downstairs.''

She raised an eyebrow. ''No computer equipment was taken? Then it could have been just kids?''

He shook his head. ''The only office broken into was Lucas's. The only game taken was his new design.''

She let that sink in. ''So any games he developed

while he worked here were the partnership's property?''

"That's right," he said. "Look, I can't imagine what any of this has to do with Lucas's disappearance. It seems pretty obvious what's going on."

She waited for him to continue because nothing seemed obvious to her.

"Since you'll probably find this out, anyway—Whiz Kidz is having a little financial trouble."

She could tell it was hard for Buzz, the original whiz kid, to admit that.

"Actually, we might have to declare bankruptcy."

"Really?" she said.

"So Lucas skipped out, taking his new game design, leaving me holding the bag." His tone reeked of bitterness.

"Did you have any insurance on the two of you in case something happened to one or the other?" she asked.

Buzz's eyes narrowed. "You think I killed him?" He laughed harshly as if the idea *had* crossed his mind. "The insurance was the first thing that had to go. Lucas's death wouldn't benefit me in any way."

So much for that theory. "What about his other games? He didn't take them?"

"Why would he? They're all dogs. Bow-wow."

She stared at him. "Not all of his games were dogs, right?"

"Well, let's just say none of Lucas's games made any real money."

"None?" She sounded like a parrot. She hoped Will was doing better than she was.

"It seems Lucas has no talent for computer

games," Buzz said even more acerbically. "And my games haven't done well enough to carry the entire business."

"What about his latest game?"

Buzz scoffed. "I don't think he was even working on a game. I think he was just stringing me along like everyone else."

"Everyone else?"

He realized his mistake. "I think Lucas might have owed money to some people."

"Why didn't you dissolve the partnership a long time ago if Lucas was such a drain?"

"The only way out of the partnership was to buy the other person out, and obviously neither of us could afford to do that."

The plot thickened. "So that's why you think he took off—because he didn't have the money to buy you out or a game that was going to bail out Whiz Kidz?"

"Oh, I think he did more than that," Buzz said. "I think he faked the break-in. He wanted everyone to think someone was after him and that he is now floating at the bottom of the Sound in cement shoes."

She didn't like that image. "Where do *you* think he is?"

"Far away from here," Buzz said, and suddenly looked angry enough to kill. "Believe me, we won't be seeing him again."

She got to her feet, afraid that was true. "You don't mind if I take a look around Lucas's office, do you?"

She could see he did mind. But for some reason his expression changed.

"There's nothing in there to see, but help yourself. It's the third door on your left."

"Let me give you my card," she said, "in case you should hear from Lucas or think of anything else that might help."

He took her card with obvious reluctance. "I won't be hearing from Lucas." Without looking at the card, he dropped it on his desk. "It's too bad about the boy, though."

"Yes," she said as she left, closing the door behind her. Down the hall she spotted Will. He gave her the high sign that he'd finished his part and pointed to a room down the hall on the right.

As she passed the third office on the left—the one Buzz had said was Lucas's—she looked in. Empty. Obviously it hadn't been used for some time, judging by the layer of dust on the desk and computer. Why had Buzz lied?

She went down the hall to where Will waited for her. "Are you sure this was Lucas's?" she whispered as she peered into the office he indicated. It had a small outer office with a slightly larger office facing the street, complete with a window.

The office was empty, as if it recently had been cleaned.

Will didn't answer, but ushered her to the elevator. Just then, the elevator doors opened and a postman started to step off. Either he wasn't used to seeing many people on this floor, or they startled him. A small square package balancing precariously on top of his load slid off. He reached for it, but missed. It hit the floor.

Will picked it up and handed it back to the embarrassed postman.

"Thanks. I guess I was gathering wool," he said, and scurried down the hall toward Buzz's office.

"So did you find anything?" Sam asked the moment they were out of the building.

"Zack's key definitely is like the ones that fit the other offices," Will said.

She looked at him in surprise. "Then how did you know that that particular one was Lucas's office?"

"Because it appears both doors were replaced after the break-in." He nodded at her surprised look. "Whoever burglarized the office must have broke down both doors."

"Does that seem odd to you?" she asked.

"Very," he said. "But since they were partners it makes sense that Lucas would have had his name on the door, right?"

"Right." She repeated what Buzz had told her. "Buzz is convinced all of this is just a stunt to allow Lucas to get out of his responsibilities." The thought scared her because of the phone message. It seemed pretty obvious now that Lucas had wanted her to take care of Zack.

"But why would Lucas go to the trouble of breaking into the building, then knocking down both doors to his office, when he still had a key?" Will asked.

"Because he didn't break into his office?" she asked, feeling a chill. "Or he did and purposely tried to make it look like a break-in. In that case, he really did stage his own disappearance, just as Buzz suspects."

Chapter Eleven

Will didn't need to ask Samantha what she believed. It was obvious she was holding out for Lucas's innocence but having a hard time based on what she'd learned about the man. He felt for her. He knew only too well what it was like to realize a person wasn't who you thought they were. Only, in his case he was learning that Samantha Murphy was a hell of a lot more woman than anything he'd imagined at the party just days before.

"Where to?" he asked, as they climbed back into the truck.

"Lucas's apartment," she said, gazing out the window as if lost in thought. Or just lost.

They drove in silence through the dense morning traffic. Lucas's apartment was in Fremont, a funky little community with brightly colored shops and interesting architecture. Samantha had an address she'd gotten from the head nurse at the Lazy Rest in Wolf Point, but couldn't be sure it wasn't old.

It turned out to be part of a gray, wood-framed four-plex on a green hillside.

Will watched the street while Samantha tried

Zack's key. The apartment door opened, and he quickly followed her inside.

A wall of stale, damp air hit him in the face. That and the distinct smell of something spoiled.

"Oh, no," he heard Samantha say in front of him.

He glanced over her shoulder as she clicked on an overhead light. The apartment had been ransacked, but since there wasn't much to trash, it wasn't too bad. The place was small and had been sparsely furnished. The bare white walls would have given it an abandoned, empty feel even if the rest of the furnishings hadn't been so minimal. Will was struck with the thought that when Lucas left here, he hadn't planned to come back.

He glanced over at Sam and saw that she'd come to the same conclusion. She tossed down a worn couch cushion she'd picked up, then swore as she stepped into the living room.

A desk dominated the room, making the couch and single chair appear out of place. Computer magazines smothered the coffee table along with several dirty coffee cups that had made dark rings on the covers. A large computer sat on the desk, but someone had broken into the back of the computer and destroyed whatever had been inside it.

"I'm going to look upstairs," Samantha said. "I thought we'd pick up some of Zack's things while we are here, if there are any left."

He glanced in the kitchen and bathroom, and then followed her up the stairs to the two bedrooms. All of Lucas's clothing was gone, his bedroom stripped of everything but the bed and bedding.

As Will looked around, he realized what had been

bothering him about this place. There weren't any nails in the walls. No dents or screw holes or faded areas where anything had hung. No framed photos or mementos gathering dust anywhere. Even the clutter looked impersonal.

Zack needs a real home, he thought, and jerked back from the idea. Sam would find him one.

He brightened as he stepped into Zack's room. It looked like a kid's space. The walls were covered with drawings and paintings, all in the hand of a child—a unique child with an active imagination.

"Hey, Zack's quite the artist," he called to Samantha, who was still searching Lucas's bedroom.

He could imagine Zack drawing this stuff. It made him feel a little better about the kid's upbringing. It also reminded him of when he used to draw a lot. It had been years since he'd drawn anything by hand. Everything was on computer now. Funny, he hadn't realized how much he missed the feel of a plain white sheet of paper or the smell of a freshly sharpened pencil.

Zack's room had been ransacked, as well. At least, he thought it had. There were clothes and toys strewn on the floor; the bed sheets were torn from the bed and all the bureau drawers were pulled out.

He noticed then that the toy box, headboard and chest of drawers all matched and looked like relics of another boy's past—no doubt Lucas's. Something about that made Will think that Lucas had cared for the boy. His feelings toward Lucas softened a little.

He went through the drawers, pulled out clothes for Zack and piled them on the bare mattress. After a moment, he sensed Samantha behind him and turned.

She stood, silhouetted against the light coming from Lucas's room. She looked so good framed like that in the doorway. Even tired and discouraged, she looked great. He knew he could be by her side in two strides, lift her into his arms and carry her to the small bed as if she were weightless.

"Did you find anything?" he asked, his voice sounding a little hoarse even to his ears.

She shook her head. "Was there something else that Zack might want us to get for him while we're here?"

He dragged his gaze from her to the room. "There are quite a few toys—mostly old, though."

She came into the room, stirring up the molecules of air around him, causing some sort of odd barometric pressure disturbance in the room as she moved to the bed to pick up the clothing he'd stacked there.

It was all he could do not to reach for her. Visions of the two of them making love glided effortlessly into his head. But not here. Not in Lucas's apartment.

When she turned, what he saw in her gaze welded him to the floor.

"Will?"

Her voice was a whisper, ragged and husky. Her eyes were a magnificent blue, as deep and warm as the Caribbean Sea. Taking a dip in them seemed inevitable—

The phone rang, jarring him out of his lascivious thoughts. Samantha seemed to start, too. She moaned softly and blinked a couple of times as if coming out of some sort of haze.

He followed her down the stairs to where the phone hung on the wall of the kitchen. She picked up the receiver on the third ring and handed it to him, mouthing, *Just say hello.*

"Hello?"

She moved close to him to listen. A fuzzy silence hummed through the line. He could feel her body heat, smell her scent.

"Who is this?" a female voice demanded.

"Who is this?" Will asked. "You called me."

"It's Mercedes. I'm looking for Lucas."

Wasn't everyone?

"Funny you should call," Samantha said, taking the phone. "I was planning to call *you.*"

MERCEDES PALMER LIVED in West Seattle in a condo overlooking Elliott Bay.

She greeted Sam and Will at the door in a god-awful brilliant red sarong. She was slim and small with a figure that had to have taken a lot of work. Her hair was cut in a pageboy and dyed a red that perfectly matched the sarong.

"I figured I'd be seeing you eventually," Lucas's second ex said resignedly.

"This is Will Sheridan," Sam said, not feeling compelled to say more—and Mercedes didn't ask. She did, however, give Will the once-over. Sam felt a pang of jealousy so strong she wanted to sock Mercedes.

"Come on in," the woman said, not sounding the least bit hospitable. They stepped in, and Sam noticed that Mercedes glanced down the street as if looking for someone. Zack? Lucas?

The condo was painted all white, the only color accent being the sarong worn by its occupant.

Mercedes motioned to a blindingly white pair of chairs by the window before she sprawled dramatically on the couch in movie-star fashion.

"So have you found him?"

"Zack or Lucas?" Sam asked as she took one of the chairs. Will sat in the other.

Mercedes frowned. "Is Zack missing, too?"

"Not anymore," she said. "Do you have any idea where Lucas is?"

"No, why ask me?"

"Because as I understand it, the ink on your divorce isn't even dry," she said.

She got the reaction she'd hoped for.

Mercedes's eyes narrowed. "Cassie, of course, told you that." She waved a hand through the air as if it didn't matter. "Lucas and I haven't lived together for months."

"Look, I don't care about your living arrangements or your divorce. I want to find Lucas. I know he's in some sort of trouble, because he wouldn't just take off and leave Zack."

The redhead seemed to study her, then Will. Will was looking around the apartment with anything but enthusiasm.

Mercedes let out a sigh and sat up, tucking her legs under her. "Did Cassie tell you that Lucas was some kind of great father?" She let out a laugh. "Always had his eyes glued to a computer screen. The boy was an absolute tear, but Lucas was too busy to tend to him. You know the kid steals?"

"I've noticed that," she admitted, not liking the picture Mercedes was painting of Lucas or Zack.

"He's incorrigible."

Again, she wondered if Mercedes was talking about Lucas or Zack. "Are you saying Lucas doesn't care about Zack?"

"Oh, I think he loved the kid in his way even under the circumstances," she said cryptically. "Which you have to admit are odd as hell."

She noted how Mercedes used the past tense when she referred to Lucas, as if he were already dead. No doubt he was to her.

"What circumstances?"

Mercedes gave her a surely-you-of-all-people-should-know look. "Lucas wasn't Zack's real father."

Sam felt the air rush out of her lungs. She gaped at Mercedes, acutely aware that Will was doing the same thing. "What?" she breathed.

Mercedes smiled, feline-like. "Cassie was pregnant with another man's baby."

The floor seemed to drop out from under Sam. Hadn't she once hoped that the baby Cassie carried wasn't Lucas's? That Cassie had tricked Lucas into marrying her? That Cassie had already been pregnant the night she went to bed with Lucas?

"That bitch," Sam said without even realizing it. "She tricked him."

Mercedes laughed, obviously pleased with the reaction. "Cassie wasn't above deceiving him into marrying her, but it wasn't like that. She made him an offer he couldn't refuse. Pretend he'd fathered her baby in exchange for everything Lucas wanted.

Money, a software business of his own, instant grat-
ification—that was Lucas.''

Sam stared at the woman openmouthed. *No.* Mercedes was just bitter. She was making this all up.
''There is no way Lucas—''

''Zack got hurt a few months ago and had to have
blood,'' Mercedes said impatiently. ''He has a rare
blood type. Lucas called Cassie, desperate because
he couldn't give the boy blood because he wasn't
related to him. Cassie didn't have the right type, either—''

Sam felt as if her heart might leap out of her chest.
''Who did?''

''That's the question, isn't it? Who is the real father of Cassie's son?''

''You don't know?'' Sam asked.

Mercedes flipped her red hair back. ''A blood do-
nor turned up, so the father was never brought in.
But I can tell you one thing—whoever he was, Cassie
really was in love with him.''

Sam found that hard to believe. ''Right.''

''Seriously, I think it's why she gave up Zack the
way she did. The kid reminded her of the guy. I
know for a fact that she'd have married him in a
heartbeat, but she found out he'd fallen head over
heels for some gal. I don't think she ever told him
about the baby.''

That didn't sound like Cassie. Sam tried to remember who her roommate had been dating back then,
but there'd been too many guys. None had lasted
long. Then a memory struck her of Cassie flirting
with Lucas's friend—

''You don't think it could be Bradley Guess?''

"Formerly known as Arnold Zingler, Buzz and nerd extraordinaire?" Mercedes shook her head. "Too geeky for her."

"Surely Lucas knew who the father was."

Mercedes smiled—pure Cheshire cat—and shook her head. "It was part of the deal. Not that Lucas *wanted* to know."

Was it possible that Lucas had really made such a deal with Cassie? Was he that desperate for money, a computer business of his own? "Why, if Zack wasn't even Lucas's, would he agree to keep the boy when Cassie left?"

"Keeping Zack was also part of the deal. Cassie wanted that part of her life behind her. Whoever Zack's father is, he broke her heart big-time."

Sam didn't like the satisfaction she heard in Mercedes's voice. She'd often wondered what kind of father Lucas was. Not the kind she'd thought, that much was obvious. She felt sick. How was it possible to be in love with a man and not even know him?

Because she'd made him up, just as Will had made her up based on a woman he saw at a party. She glanced at Will. Talk about a pair of fools!

"How do you know this?" she asked shakily, wondering if she was the only one they'd kept in the dark, the only one they'd betrayed.

"I didn't find out until after I married the jerk. Just like I didn't know about his gambling problem or what that kid was like."

"Gambling?"

Mercedes smiled as if to say, *What kind of detective are you, anyway?* "Surely you know about his online trading?"

"I'd heard he might have been in a little over his head."

Mercedes snorted. "When people come to your door to break your legs, you're in a little more than over your head."

"Did someone come to break his legs?" she asked, trying to keep the shock out of her voice.

Mercedes waved a hand through the air again as if big burly men were always knocking at the door wanting to hurt Lucas over his debts.

"Is that why you divorced him?"

"One of many reasons," the faux redhead said, not bothering to hide her bitterness. "Lucas kept expecting me to bail him out. Funny how he only married women with money, don't you think?"

The words stung. Sam's family wasn't rich, but they weren't poor, either. Obviously she hadn't had enough to offer Lucas.

"I cut my losses and got the hell out," Mercedes was saying. "Are you happy now that you know the whole ugly story?"

Not really. But *did* she know the whole story? Cassie had said Zack was the problem between Mercedes and Lucas, and that it had been Mercedes who wanted more money in the divorce settlement. But it seemed Mercedes had her own money. Or a boyfriend with money.

Sam glanced around. The condo was certainly posh and had a view of the water. And Mercedes didn't look as if she were headed for the poorhouse. That dye job alone must have set her back a good hundred and fifty.

"Then you think Lucas is on the lam because of his debts?" she asked.

Mercedes shrugged as if she couldn't care less. "I wouldn't be surprised if he turned up in the Sound wearing concrete slippers."

Sam shivered, feeling as cold as the frigid decor. That was the second time today someone had suggested that scenario. But Mercedes's lack of interest in Lucas's fate chilled her more. Worse yet was the woman's lack of interest in Zack. She hadn't even asked about the boy.

Sam glanced over at Will. He looked a little cold himself. Then a thought struck her. "Why did you call Lucas's apartment today if you knew he was missing?"

"Because of the damn package I just got in the mail," Mercedes snapped, and got up to retrieve a small square white box from the top of the desk in the corner. "He's not involving me in any of his deals. Not again. I don't want anything to do with whatever he's up to this time."

She practically threw the box at Sam, and then dusted off her hands as if she felt dirty just touching it. She went back to her original position on the couch. "It's all yours," she said. "After all, you're the detective, right? So find Lucas and tell him to go straight to hell. And if you should see Cassie— Never mind. I'd rather tell her myself."

That was succinct enough.

Sam folded back the flaps on the box, not surprised to see a computer CD game box inside, the name Catastrophe painted across the black cover in what looked like blood.

Just as Cassie had said, there was a note included. It read,

> In case something should happen to me, and you receive this package, take the CD to the police and tell them it is one of five pieces. They will understand why the game is so important once they put the pieces together. For your own safety, do not keep this piece of the game.

Cryptic as a computer game.

"I can't imagine why he'd send anything to me," Mercedes was saying.

Sam couldn't, either.

"Just get it out of here," the redhead said. "I'm sick to death of Lucas's games."

Sam got up, feeling it was time to go. Will was already on his feet.

"Any idea who got the other pieces?" he asked.

Mercedes swung her gaze over to him. She seemed to soften. Or maybe it was just Sam's imagination.

"No, nor do I care."

"Cassie seems to think the game might be worth millions," Samantha said, throwing out a little bait.

Mercedes snorted. "Greed is such an ugly trait. Cassie has already tried to buy my piece from me."

It definitely was time to go. "Thanks for your help. If you hear anything—"

"I won't," Mercedes said, not bothering to get up. "Lucas knows better than to call me."

"I suppose you're right."

Will opened the door for them, and Sam hurried out, thankful for the warmth of the rainy day outside.

She practically raced down the steps, running from Mercedes's uncaring coldness, running from the image the woman had painted of Lucas. Was it possible he was an uninterested father, a man who married only for money and a compulsive gambler in over his head?

She could forgive him for a lot. Even for betraying her love five years ago to make a deal with the devil. But how could he betray a boy he'd raised as his own son? How could he put Zack in danger?

Chapter Twelve

Will didn't know what to say as he followed Samantha to the pickup. She was obviously upset. He knew that having him here didn't help matters. It was one thing to be jilted; it was another to learn that the jilter had done it for money. If that were true.

"Mercedes might have a reason to lie," he said, an understatement if ever there was one.

"Too bad it had a ring of truth to it, huh?" she said as she climbed into the truck and looked out at Elliott Bay.

The dark gray water didn't do much to pick up the mood. Nor could Will think of anything to say to make Sam feel better. All he could do as he started the pickup was damn Lucas O'Brien, wherever he was. It didn't seem enough, under the circumstances.

"I feel like a fool," Samantha said in a small voice after they'd driven a few miles.

He laughed. "We've all been there." He glanced over at her.

She returned his smile with a tentative one of her own. "What a jerk."

"He couldn't have been all bad," Will heard himself say. "Look at Zack. He's a good kid. He needs a little guidance, but he'll be okay."

Her smile broadened. "He is a great kid, isn't he?" She sobered. "If Lucas isn't Zack's natural father, then who is? Not only could Cassie come forward and try to take Zack, but so could his father."

He nodded, having already thought of that when they were in the Ice Tomb with Princess Mercedes. "It seems pretty obvious why Cassie wants Zack after all this time. If the father suddenly appears—"

"Lucas's stupid game," Samantha said, looking down at the box resting in her lap. "Damn Lucas."

He seconded that emotion as he drove back toward the city, wondering what to do next. They seemed to have run out of leads, and were running out of time, as well. The more they learned, the deeper in trouble Zack seemed to be. Will tried not to think about Zack waiting for them back at Charley's, or the bike he'd promised the boy. He couldn't bear the thought of turning the kid over to the authorities. He had a suspicion that the moment they did, Cassie would suddenly materialize. Or Zack's father would show up with proof of paternity.

"Five pieces of the game," Samantha said. "Cassie and Mercedes each got one. That leaves three."

A memory came to him like a lightbulb going on in his head as he glanced at the small white box in her lap. "How was that package sent?"

She glanced down. "It looks like it came by Special Delivery."

"Remember the postman we passed in the hallway at Whiz Kidz? The box he dropped when we startled him at the elevator?"

She sat up a little. "I remember. You picked it up and handed it to him."

Will nodded. "It could have been the twin to the one you're holding."

"Tell me it was addressed to Bradley Guess."

"No," he said, suddenly deflated. "It was addressed to someone named Arnold something."

"Arnold Zingler?"

"Yeah," he said, and looked over at her. "I take it you know him?"

"Guess! He changed his name to Bradley Guess when he and Lucas started Whiz Kidz. In college everyone called him Buzz. So he got a copy of the game? How about that? Three down, two to go."

She sounded a little more upbeat. He wished he felt the same way.

He pulled up to a stop sign and rubbed the back of his neck. Why did he feel as if he was waiting for the other shoe to drop?

SAM FELT A SURGE of new hope. Lucas had sent a copy of the game to his partner. Not under his new name, but under the one Lucas had known him by back in college. Did that have any significance? She thought it might. Especially if Lucas suspected Buzz might be Zack's father.

She recalled how Buzz hadn't enquired about Zack, and felt cold inside. What had he said as she was leaving? Something like, *"It's too bad about the boy."* Now those words seemed to take on added meaning.

She stared out at the rainy day, all the more determined to protect Zack, no matter what. She pulled out her cell phone to call Charley and see how Zack was doing, and remembered that she'd turned it off while she was in Mercedes's condo.

She had a message. *Cassie?* Until that moment, she hadn't realized that she'd been waiting for Cassie to call again. Sam knew Cassie would be looking for Lucas and the game pieces. So Sam was sure she'd be hearing from her former roommate. Only this time, Sam was looking forward to the confrontation. It had been coming for five years.

But the message was from Charley, and it was urgent.

"Charley called," she told Will as she hurriedly dialed the number, her fingers shaking.

Charley answered on the first ring, and she knew by the tone of his voice that something was terribly wrong.

"Is Zack—"

"Zack's fine," he said quickly. "They just pulled a car from the Sound, Sam. There was a body inside, pretty decomposed."

She held her breath, knowing what he was going to say.

"They have a positive ID. It's Lucas O'Brien. The car is registered to him and the identification found on the body is his, as well. He'd been shot twice at close range with a .38."

Just like Al.

"The coroner thinks the body has been in the water since Friday."

The day Zack was kidnapped. The day Lucas disappeared. He's been dead this whole time.

She closed her eyes, squeezing the phone tightly.

She couldn't have seen him on the ferry, after all. "Did you tell Zack?"

"No, I figured you'd want to do that."

"We'll be right there."

ONE LOOK AT HER and Will's heart took off at a sprint. "Has something happened to Zack?"

"It's Lucas."

He listened as she related what Charley had told her.

"I'm sorry, Sam," he said, feeling at a loss as to how to help her.

"Amazing how people pass through our lives, some of them barely making a ripple, and others—"

She shook her head again and he reached for her, knowing exactly what she meant. Samantha Murphy was one of those people who'd made more than a ripple in his life. And for a man who liked smooth waters— He pulled over and drew her to him. She buried her face in his shoulder, and he cradled her in his arms and damned Lucas O'Brien's soul.

"We need to tell Zack," she said into his shirt.

He nodded, and she sat up, straightening and drying her eyes. He got the pickup going again and headed for the ferry, sick at heart for Zack. And Samantha.

CHARLEY MET HER at the door and hugged her tightly. "You all right?"

She nodded. He seemed to study her, and she knew he was wondering how she could still care for a guy like Lucas O'Brien. She couldn't have explained her feelings to him any more than she could to herself. She'd loved a man she thought was Lucas, and that man had died for her long before his body was pulled from the Sound.

She'd cried less for that loss than for Zack's. He'd lost his father. Even if Lucas hadn't been his biological father. Even if Lucas hadn't been a great father. Zack had lost the only father he'd known.

"Where is he?" she asked.

Charley motioned toward the family room at the end of the hall. She could hear laughter and the sound of some sort of toy. As she neared, she saw that they played with a large racetrack. Tiny cars careered along the track, some flying off occasionally to a roar of laughter.

"Zack—?"

She felt Will's large, warm hand on her back. It sent a surge of something strong and powerful through her, something she didn't dare put a name to.

"Will and I need to talk to you a moment."

Zack frowned and instantly looked anxious. At least he'd had a few short hours to play and be a five-year-old without the weight of the world on his small shoulders.

"What is it?" he asked in a tiny voice.

"Come on, kids," Charley said. "I need your help." His children groaned and complained as Charley herded them out of the room and closed the door behind them.

Zack looked up at her, his brown eyes filled with worry.

"I have some bad news," she said, kneeling to take his thin shoulders in her hands. "Your dad—"

"He isn't coming back, is he?" Zack said, and looked up at Will.

"No, son," Will said. "He isn't."

The boy swallowed, tears pooling in his eyes as he nodded. "I didn't think so."

She drew him into her arms and hugged his small, frail body tightly. "I'm so sorry, Zack." His body felt stiff in her arms, as if he might break if she hugged him too hard. She pulled back to look into his face. Pain darkened his eyes; his lower lip quivered. He was trying so hard not to cry. Trying so hard to be that tough-guy. Her heart broke just looking at him.

"Oh, Zack—"

She shot Will a pleading look.

Oh, hell. He swallowed the lump in his throat and nodded. She stood and moved back.

Will pulled up a chair, sick at heart at the sight of the little boy standing in the middle of the room. He sat down and motioned for Zack to join him, realizing he was in way over his head here. What did he know about kids—let alone handling something like this? But he saw himself in Zack, in the way the child was trying so hard to be strong.

"You all right?"

Zack nodded and moved toward him slowly.

"I lost my father when I was a kid, too," he said conversationally.

Zack's eyes widened a little. "Really?"

Will nodded. "I was nine, though, so I was older than you are. I remember trying really hard not to cry."

Zack didn't say anything, but he inched closer.

"I wanted to cry but I thought I had to be tough, you know."

The boy nodded and came to stand at the edge of the overstuffed chair. "My daddy had to go away," Zack said solemnly.

Will looked at the boy, afraid to move or breathe or speak for fear Zack might not say any more. "I'm sorry about that." It was all he could think to say.

Tears pooled in Zack's eyes. "He said I had to be strong and brave."

Will thought his heart would break. "You are definitely a strong, brave kid, I can tell you that."

The boy looked up at him for confirmation.

Will nodded.

He could see Zack's lower lip trembling, the tears spilling— He glanced up at Samantha, but she motioned for him to keep going. He pulled the boy up on his lap and surrounded him with his arms. The rigid little body began to soften, then to jerk with gut-wrenching sobs that Will suspected the boy had been holding back for a long time.

Will just held him in his arms and rubbed the trembling back with the flat of his hand.

After a while, Zack straightened and rubbed at his swollen red eyes. "Are *you* ever scared?" he asked in a little-boy voice.

"Are you kidding? I've been so scared sometimes my knees knock."

Zack stared at him, disbelieving.

"Sometimes I think I'm going to throw up. Or cry."

The boy looked skeptical.

"Everyone cries when they're hurt or sad. Even me. And everyone is afraid sometimes. Even Sam."

Zack really wasn't buying *that*. "My daddy's not coming back ever?"

"No, Zack, he's not. But I do know that he'd come back if he could, and I think you know that, too, right?"

Zack nodded.

"Don't worry, okay? Sam will take care of everything. She's an amazing woman. What guy wouldn't want a woman like Sam looking out for him?" He realized what he'd said and looked toward the door and Sam.

Her gaze locked with his, her eyes wide like a deer caught in headlights.

Only a guy who didn't have a lick of sense, he thought. Or a guy looking for a wife, a certain type of wife, one who didn't carry a gun or steal kids or put herself into danger all the time.

"So," he said to Zack, "everything's going to be all right." He doubted that as he glanced toward the doorway again. Sam was gone.

SAMANTHA STOOD OUTSIDE the door for several moments. What *would* happen to Zack? She couldn't bear to think. When she heard them coming, she hurriedly tried to pull herself together. The last thing she wanted Will to see was the hurt in her eyes. Of course he didn't want her. He didn't even want to date her now that he knew she wasn't who he'd thought she was.

You're not falling for the guy, are you?

Good heavens, no. What do you think I am, stupid?

"Is Zack all right?" Charley asked, peering down the hallway at her.

She straightened and put on her best face. "Will's talking to him. They've become pretty close." Tears threatened. She willed them away. "I'm scared for him. Whoever's determined to get that game will feel they need Zack now if they hope to force me to find the pieces for them."

Charley nodded. "Have you talked to Lucas's next of kin?"

She stared at him. "You mean his grandmother Gladdie?"

"No, his brother."

"Lucas has a brother?" Had she known *anything* about Lucas? Or had it all been a lie? He'd told her he had no one but his grandmother.

"He has a half-brother who lives here," Charley said as the hallway door opened behind her. "We stumbled across him when we began investigating the break-in at Whiz Kidz."

She turned to see Zack and Will.

"Can I go play with the kids now?" Zack asked.

"Sure, you can," she said, patting his shoulder as he passed.

Her gaze lifted to Will's. He looked as sheepish and as embarrassed as she felt.

"Lucas's half-brother identified the items found on the body as Lucas's," Charley said, after the kids had all raced back into the family room and slammed the door behind them.

Will expressed surprise. "I thought Gladdie was his only living relative."

"So did I. It seems there's a lot about Lucas I didn't know," she said, hearing the bitterness in her voice. "What is this brother's name, and how do I find him?"

ERIC ROSS LIVED in the University District just off Auburn Street in a run-down apartment house that smelled of cooked cabbage.

The man who answered the door bore little resemblance to Lucas, except for the eyes. They were that same pale green. Nothing like Zack's dark brown eyes.

He held a can of beer in his fist and looked as if it wasn't his first.

"Eric Ross?" Samantha enquired.

"Yeah?" He regarded them warily as if they might be bill collectors.

"Who is it?" asked a rather shrill female voice from the other room.

"I don't know yet," he called back, sounding irritated.

"I'm Samantha Murphy, a private investigator. I'm investigating your brother's death."

Eric opened his mouth to speak, then closed it again. He appeared shaken and a little disoriented. Then he hurriedly brushed his hands on his jeans and offered her a hand. "Come in, please, come in."

She took his hand and shook it quickly, before he offered it to Will. "This is Will Sheridan. My... colleague."

Eric ushered them into a cramped little room full

of hard-used furniture. "Sit down, please, sit down."
He seemed embarrassed by the room and the blonde
in it.

The young woman looked like a girl, thin and
boney, small-breasted and big-eyed. She wore only
a large, oversize T-shirt. A pair of scrawny legs stuck
out the bottom, ending in bare feet. She looked at
Sam and Will, and frowned.

"Bebe, do you mind?" Eric snapped.

Bebe. Where had Sam heard that name?

Bebe gave them a curious look, then turned and
casually left the room, leaving the bedroom door partially open. No doubt so she could hear the conversation while she dressed.

"It isn't what you think," Eric said.

Sam wasn't sure what she thought as she sat down
on the edge of the blanket-covered sofa, and Will
took a chair with a view of the doorway. She wondered if he'd done that on purpose. He looked uncomfortable, as if he had reason to be wary.

Eric sat on a straight-back chair across from the
couch. He looked nervous and kept glancing toward
the bedroom where Bebe had disappeared.

"Do you have any idea why someone would want
to kill Lucas?" Sam asked.

Eric looked surprised by the question. "The game,
of course." He looked again toward the bedroom.
"What other reason could there be?"

She wished she knew. "Which game is that?" she
asked, wondering how much Lucas had told his half-
brother.

Eric looked confused. "The one the cops said he
was working on."

"He didn't talk about the game with you?" she asked.

Eric shrugged. "He mentioned he was working on something big. But he always said that."

"He didn't mention that he thought someone might want to kill him?"

"Not to me."

"Did you ever see the game?" she asked.

He shook his head. "He didn't let anyone see his games until they were on the market. Paranoid, you know."

"So you don't even know if this game, that was supposedly really big, even exists?" she asked.

He frowned. "It must exist. Why else is Lucas dead?"

It still sounded unbelievable that Lucas could have been killed over a computer game.

"I thought you said it was *more* than a game?" Bebe said from the bedroom doorway.

Isn't that what the hype on the game boxes all said? "In what way?" Sam asked.

"Don't listen to her," Eric interrupted. "She doesn't know what she's talking about."

"But you said what Lucas did was the *ultimate* game," Bebe pouted. She'd pulled on a pair of too-large, holey jeans. "Mailing out pieces of it the way he did."

Eric made a face at her that any fool could see meant shut up.

"So you got a piece of the game?" Sam said, looking to Eric.

"No," he said shaking his head adamantly. "Why

would he send me a piece and involve me in this mess?"

"Because you're his half-brother," Sam pointed out. "If you didn't get a piece of the game, then how did you know that Lucas had mailed them out?"

Eric frowned. He looked to Bebe as if she had the answer. "The cops," he said finally. "The cops must have mentioned it when they questioned me about Lucas's death. Yeah, that's right, they said he mailed out five pieces of the game to friends or something."

Sam considered that for a moment. "I heard he gambled online and could have gotten involved with loan sharks," she said, fishing.

"Who told you that?" Eric demanded. "It wasn't true. Not Lucas." But he didn't sound very convincing.

"Then who do you think killed him for the game?" she asked.

"Someone as brilliant as Lucas was bound to have enemies," he said with a shrug.

Something in his tone caught Sam's attention. "Are you also in the game software business?"

"Yeah," Eric said avoiding her gaze. "Nothing like Lucas, mind you. I just kinda dabble in it."

"You'll sell a game someday," Bebe said, as she came in and perched on the arm of the couch. "Eric's got real talent."

He looked embarrassed to have her suddenly fawning over him.

Bebe leaned toward them. "You know if Lucas had helped Eric even a little, Eric would be bigger in the business than Lucas ever thought about being."

"Bebe," Eric warned.

"It's true, come on," she said, waving him off with a hand. "Lucas was just so full of himself. He even said one time that he was going to come up with software that could break into any computer in the world and steal anything he wanted without anyone knowing who he was or even suspecting he'd been there until it was too late. Any computer in the world. Can you imagine that kind of arrogance?"

"Bebe, get me a beer," Eric snapped.

It was obvious Bebe didn't like being ordered around. Nor did she want to leave the room, but she did, although reluctantly.

"Don't pay her any mind," he said the moment she was gone. "She's just a game designer groupie. She believes anything you tell her." He didn't look happy about that. "Catastrophe is just a game."

Catastrophe. She thought he'd said he didn't know anything about the game—including its name.

"So did you get a piece of the game?" Bebe asked Sam, as she came back into the room, holding an open can of beer.

"No," Sam said. Or Andy, her associate at the office, would have called to tell her. No, Lucas hadn't sent her a piece. He'd just left her a message on her answering machine telling her to take care of—something. Someone. Zack, obviously. "How about you?"

"Me?" Bebe cried. "Lucas wouldn't give me the time of day!"

"Who do you think does have a piece of it?" Sam asked, watching Bebe.

Bebe shrugged as she handed Eric the beer and

sloshed some of the brew onto the carpet. He gave her a dirty look as she rubbed the spilled liquid into the rug with her bare foot.

"So what's in it for you?" Bebe asked her pointedly.

"I just want to find out who killed Lucas and why," Sam said.

"Got any ideas?" Bebe asked.

Sam shook her head and looked over at Will. They'd hit another wall. Then she remembered the credit card she'd found in Zack's backpack. "Do you know anyone named Robert Walker?"

"Bobby?" Bebe cried. "Sure, he invested in Lucas's game. Wouldn't invest in any of Eric's though."

"Shut up, Bebe," Eric snapped, this time more forcefully. "How do you know Bob?" he asked Sam.

"I just heard his name somewhere," she said vaguely, and shrugged as if it didn't matter, but she watched Bebe's face. The girl's gaze flicked nervously to Eric, but she said nothing as Sam reluctantly followed Will out the door.

"You think she'll be all right?" Will asked, obviously referring to Bebe.

Sam glanced back to see Bebe trying to make up to Eric, cuddling against him and talking fast. "I hope so. What bothers me is why Eric was lying about having a piece of the game," she said as Will opened her side of the pickup and she slipped in. "Charley told me that the cops didn't mention the name of the game or that there were five pieces mailed out. The only way Eric could have known that was if he got one—and the note with it.''

ROBERT WALKER was playing tennis under a large white bubble in his impressive backyard. He wiped his face with a towel before coming over. He was a handsome, athletic man in obviously good shape.

''You must be Samantha Murphy,'' he said congenially as he offered a hand. His handshake was firm, his gaze steady and strong. He didn't look like the kind of man who would know Eric, let alone Bebe. Nor did he look like a man who went by ''Bobby.'' ''My secretary said you'd be dropping by.''

''This is my associate, Will Sheridan.''

If Eric or Bebe had called to warn him, he didn't show it.

He shook Will's hand. ''Can I offer you something to drink? Juice? Or something stronger?''

''No, thanks,'' she said, and Will declined, as well. ''I just wanted to ask you some questions about Whiz Kidz, the computer game company you invested in.''

Bobby frowned but motioned to the lounge chairs along the edge of the covered court. A sleek, lean woman continued to hit balls from a machine at the other end of the huge building.

''Whiz Kidz? The name doesn't mean anything to me. I've invested in a lot of companies. I don't have much firsthand knowledge of their day-to-day operations,'' Bobby said.

''I'm mostly interested in Lucas O'Brien, a computer game designer and one of the partners in Whiz Kidz.''

She could tell the name rang a bell.

"Oh. Lucas. Sure." He turned to watch the woman on the court smack a few balls before he looked at the two of them again. "I really don't understand why you'd be interested in my investments."

"Lucas was in partnership with Whiz Kidz. It was in financial trouble. So was Lucas."

Bobby smiled. "A lot of small computer businesses in Seattle are just getting on their feet. It takes a while in the game business. The average computer game sells twenty thousand copies—the successful game, one-hundred thousand. Less than one percent of the games written sell more than one-hundred thousand copies." He held up his hands. "It's a tough industry. You have to be very clever to survive."

"And Lucas was clever?"

Bobby grinned.

"How much can a successful game make?" Will asked.

"A megahit? Three-hundred thousand dollars a month for a year, maybe more."

"Wow, I didn't realize there was that kind of money in games," Will said.

"You'd be surprised. It's just a matter of finding the right game at the right time. The game market is incredible," Bobby said enthusiastically.

"I guess I'm surprised you'd invest in a company that hadn't had a hit game in five years," Sam said.

He smiled. "I didn't invest in Whiz Kidz. I invested in Lucas O'Brien. The top games are being designed by guys with about seven years of experience. That's what it takes to know if you have a game that's going to work. Lucas was at that point. Plus, he had something he was working on that interested me.''

''Really?'' she said. ''This game he was working on was separate from his partnership with Whiz Kidz?'' She wondered if Buzz knew this.

Bobby nodded. ''He wanted to do something different, something on his own.''

''He told you about the game?''

''Not a lot—just that he thought he had something. That was good enough for me. I usually go on my gut feelings with these things.'' He glanced around the tennis court. ''So far, it's paid off.''

She was sure now that neither Eric nor Bebe had called to warn Bobby about her. Probably didn't want to admit that they'd been the ones who'd told her about him.

''How did you find out about Lucas and his game, to invest in the project?'' she asked.

Bobby looked surprised.

''I mean,'' she continued, ''it sounds like Lucas was pretty hush-hush about the game.''

He nodded and seemed to be searching for the answer. ''I don't remember. Probably a mutual friend.''

That didn't seem likely, and they both knew it.

''You didn't happen to lose a credit card recently, did you?'' she asked.

He looked startled. ''As a matter of fact, one of mine was stolen—''

She pulled the card from her purse and handed it to him. ''I just happened to find it on the ground.''

A whopper of a lie, but no telling where Zack—or Ralph—had picked it up.

"Thanks for returning it," Bobby said, and laid it on the table between them. "But I'd already called it in and canceled it."

If he was lying, he was better than she was.

She wasn't sure how to give him the news. But his arrogance made it a little easier. "I just spoke with the police. Lucas O'Brien was found murdered. He'd been floating in the Sound since Friday when his office was broken into."

Bobby blanched. "He's dead?"

She nodded and waited for him to ask about the game. He didn't.

"Lucas didn't happen to send you a piece of the game he was working on, did he?" she asked.

"No, why?" He looked to Will.

"It's missing," Will said.

Bobby didn't say anything, but he didn't look quite as tanned as before. She and Will got to their feet. Bobby Walker seemed relieved they were leaving. Maybe he really was only upset over Lucas's death and not worried about his investment. Or maybe he had a piece of the game and planned to get the others.

"I hope you didn't invest too much," she said conversationally.

Bobby smiled and shook his head as he picked up his racket. "Not all investments pay off. You have to just take the bad with the good."

"I guess so," she said, and she and Will left.

Behind them, inside the bubble, the bouncing balls stopped and there was loud cursing, followed by what sounded like a tennis racket shattering on a hard surface.

It wasn't until Will was driving away that Sam remembered where she'd heard the name Bebe before. Bradley Guess, aka Buzz Zingler, had been talking to someone on the phone he called Bebe.

Chapter Thirteen

It was growing dark by the time he and Samantha caught the ferry to Vashon Island. A cold wet wind whipped the top of the water, sending spray into the air like driving rain. Will was glad they'd stayed in the pickup. The Sound seemed dark and treacherous.

Samantha looked exhausted from lack of sleep, he noticed.

When her cell phone rang, he started, suddenly struck with an irrational fear. "Don't answer it."

She jerked her head up in surprise. "It might be Charley." She snapped on the phone and put it to her ear, her gaze never leaving his face, as if she didn't know what to make of him.

He watched her eyes widen, then fill with tears. "I know" was all she said before she clicked off again.

He closed his eyes, not wanting to hear.

"It *was* Charley. Cassie got a court order. She's taken custody of Zack."

"This quickly? How is that possible?" Will demanded.

"Her father is rather influential in the state of Washington, it seems," Sam said.

"I'm so sorry." Sorrier than she could ever know. He felt sick inside. And mad.

"Oh, Will," she moaned, her eyes fresh with tears. "Charley says there is nothing we can do without proof that Cassie was involved in Al's death. And even that will take time."

He leaned toward her, desperately wanting to take her in his arms and kiss away the hurt. He searched for words to reassure her. They were still missing two copies of Lucas's damn game. But they had a hell of a lot of suspects. "She can't do anything without all of the game pieces," he said. "She still needs you to find the rest of them. And eventually, she will need the one Mercedes gave you."

Samantha swallowed and sleeved away the tears shimmering on her lashes. "You're right. Cassie wants the game. That's why she's taken Zack. She'll take good care of him."

Until she gets what she wants.

He brushed back a strand of hair from her face. She was so beautiful, her eyes glowing with tears and determination. Damn but he wanted to make love to her—as if that would make everything better.

His gaze moved over her face, lighting on her mouth, her luscious mouth, the memory of their kisses still fresh in his mind.

She shifted on the seat, her lips a whisper away from his. He could feel her breath, hear her sudden rapid breathing, see the pulse in her temple throbbing. Her eyes widened and darkened.

Someone moved past the pickup. She jerked back. "Sorry," she whispered.

Not half as sorry as he was. He took a breath and let it out slowly. "Yeah," he said, and cracked his window a little. It felt too hot in the pickup, her nearness unnerving, his body on overload. He'd hoped in the days he'd spent with her that the attraction would lessen. It hadn't. If anything, he wanted her more with each passing hour. His body ached with a need he knew only she could satisfy. He wanted her in his arms. To feel the warmth of her body pressed against his. To touch his lips to the throbbing pulse at her temple. To cup her cheek in his hand. To kiss her and taste her and ultimately make love to her, slowly and gently—

"Will?"

He fought off the image of Samantha naked in his arms and sat up straighter. "Yeah?"

"It sounds like we're almost there," she said. "I'll be right back. I just need a little fresh air."

He wanted to warn her to be careful, but she was already out of the pickup and gone. As if he had to warn her.

He sat for a moment, cursing to himself. How had he let himself get into such an impossible situation? If Sam were anything but a private investigator— He got out of the pickup and went after her.

SHE STUMBLED up to the deck, needing the air and the cold and darkness to hide her tears, to sort out her thoughts. She'd almost kissed him. Again. Only this time would have been different. This time there would have been no holding back. Her heart raced with the thought of being in his arms.

You know it would only be temporary.

I know. But I don't care. I want him. I need him.

I thought you weren't going to let yourself need any man after Lucas?

The ferry slowed. Ahead, the lights of the island glittered like jewels along the shoreline. She worked her way to the back where the deck was empty. Standing at the railing, she looked out across the water. Mist rolled up out of the darkness and a breeze whipped the inky surface of the water. *Will.* Her mind wrapped about his name the way she wanted to wrap her arms around him; her body ached for him with a desire like none she had ever known.

Even for Lucas. Not like this.

She'd become accustomed to the sound of Will's voice, to his smile, to the way he took off his glasses and cleaned them when he was thinking. Just the mere brush of his fingers against her skin—

She shivered and hugged herself against the cold night and the thought of never knowing Will's touch the way she wanted to.

I've fallen in love with him!

Dumb move.

No kidding.

She was destined to lose both Will and Zack. What had she been thinking, letting either of them get so close? Worse, she'd found herself daydreaming about giving Zack the home he so desperately needed, and she'd seen Will in that perfect little family photo. What *had* she been thinking? To even let herself dream that dream again—

She saw something move, and thought it had to be Will. He'd come up on deck after her. Her heart leapt. But only for an instant. Instead of Will's handsome face, she caught a glimpse of blond hair sticking out of a dark hood. The next moment she felt hands grab her and push hard.

She slammed into the railing, losing her balance and her footing on the wet deck. She felt the hands again. Strong hands. Grabbing her purse. Forcing her overboard!

WILL MADE HIS WAY UP to the deck, the night air wet and cold against his face. They were almost to shore. Where was she? He'd gone from feeling foolish and angry with himself to feeling anxious about Sam. He'd come along on this ride to watch over her. Now he'd let her take off into the night, alone and hurt. And he'd been the one to hurt her.

But he couldn't give her what she wanted. And they both knew it. He couldn't be married to a private investigator. He couldn't live each day knowing she might be jeopardizing her life. Worse, he couldn't have the family he desperately wanted. Now more than ever. Zack and Samantha had shown him how much he wanted children and a wife. Not a P.I.

But tell that to his heart. To his aching body that right now only wanted to hold Samantha against him and breathe in the scent of her. Right now, he'd have promised her anything, just to feel her safe in his arms.

He had started toward the back of the ferry and was working his way along the railing when he saw her—and the cloaked figure trying to push her overboard!

He called out and ran down the deck. But he could see that Samantha had been taken by surprise. She was off balance, slipping on the wet deck, the figure overpowering her.

"No!" he cried.

But it was too late. Samantha went over the rail and dropped out of sight.

The hooded figure had heard him, and, without turning, raced up the other side of the deck, disappearing behind the passenger cabin.

He heard Sam's cry as she fell, then the splash as she hit the water. He reached the edge of the deck, shrugging out of his jacket as he climbed the railing and dove into the dark water after her.

LATER SHE WOULDN'T REMEMBER anything but the cold and darkness. And the shock. Falling through the black. Then the icy water. Hitting hard, going under and under. The fear.

At first she'd thought she'd only dreamed Will's arms dragging her to the surface. Powerful arms. His body the only warmth. His reassuring words as he pulled her with him to safety.

It wasn't until much later, wrapped in a blanket, sitting in the front of the pickup, that she understood what had happened. She'd been pushed overboard. Her purse with Mercedes's game piece had been stolen. Cassie had stolen the CD and pushed her.

That's when the shaking had started, her body convulsing from it, and not even Will's strong arms could stop the trembling.

"You saved my life," she said, her teeth chattering as he lifted her into his arms. "Again."

"Don't think about it," he whispered back.

Where was he taking her? Not to Charley's. Too far, he'd said. A motel cottage on the beach.

"She tried to kill me." Sam hadn't seen her face. Just a glimpse of the blond hair. "Cassie tried to kill me."

Will carried her into the cottage and kicked the door closed behind them, Sam still wrapped in the blanket he'd gotten from someone on the ferry. He didn't turn on the lights, didn't stop at the bed—just carried her straight to the shower and turned it on.

She was crying now, burying her face against his neck, aware of his wet clothing, aware that he'd jumped into the water after her. This incredible man whom she'd once thought was predictable. "Will," she whispered, and pressed her body as close as the blanket and their clothing would allow. "Will."

He leaned her against the shower wall as he stripped off her wet clothing. Then, still clothed, he stepped into the warm spray with her. She leaned against him, her mouth seeking his, his kisses wet and warm and openmouthed.

"Will," she whispered against his mouth. "Will."

He must have heard the plea in her voice, felt the insistence of her kisses, of her naked body against his. "Sam, I don't think—"

She covered his mouth with her own, swallowing his words. "Don't think," she whispered, turning her face up to his, the spray catching in her lashes, the water making her slick and pink and delectable. "Not now."

HE COULD FEEL the heat coming back into her body, and the strength returning. She leaned up to take his mouth again, her kiss demanding. He held her to him, afraid to let her go, still shocked by what had happened. What *could* have happened if he hadn't gotten to her when he did.

But she was safe. Safe. He closed his eyes and ran his hands over her slick, smooth curves. *Don't do this. You can't give her what she wants. What she needs.*

But he could no more let go of her than he could imagine waking up tomorrow and not seeing her, not hearing her voice, not smelling her intoxicating scent.

"Will."

He opened his eyes.

She gazed up at him, the darkness gone from the blue-green, her body no longer trembling from the cold or fear, but from desire. It flashed in her eyes like sunlight on a tropical sea.

"Make love to me," she whispered.

He swore softly, all the fight gone out of him. He knew it was wrong; he knew they'd both regret it in the morning. Especially Sam. But he covered her mouth with his, deepening the kiss, needing her as much as she thought she needed him.

She stripped off his wet clothing, kissing the cool flesh beneath, leaving behind a hot, sensuous trail with her lips until he was as naked as she was.

They clung to each other, their bodies slippery and wet and warm from the water and desire. Steam rose in the shower, cloaking them in a surreal mist that made his head swim and his body weak with the need to be inside her.

He turned off the water just before it grew cold, and swung her up into his arms. In two strides, he carried her to the bed. For a moment, he looked down at her, his eyes trailing over her naked skin slowly, lovingly. His gaze met hers, and a current sparked between them as hot and bright as flames.

''God, you're beautiful,'' he whispered.

Samantha felt herself flush, the heat racing through her veins, making her throb with a need for him. She reached up and touched his cheek, cupping it in her hand. Slowly she pulled him down.

He covered one hard, ripe nipple with his mouth, gently sucking it to an aching point. She groaned with pleasure, arching her body to the warm wetness of his wonderful mouth. He drew the other nipple in and taunted it to a hard peak with his tongue, sending a hot wave to her center.

She ran her hands over his muscled chest, across the hard contours of his back and shoulders, her fingers memorizing every inch with her touch. She knew she couldn't have Will Sheridan. Not the way she wanted him—forever. But she could have him tonight. And that was enough.

He explored her body, finding every erotic spot as if with a sixth sense. She surrendered to him, giving herself in a way she never had before. And never would again.

His touch made her implode deep inside with shudders that sent goose bumps racing across her bare skin. Then he took her in his arms and kissed her crazy before he slowly, tenderly, filled her, fulfilled her.

She rocked with their rhythm, like a boat in the waves, their lovemaking a music that drifted on the night breeze as waves lapped at the shore. She cried out his name again and again, until finally he filled her with heat and contentment and collapsed in her arms. She held him to her, feeling the weight of him, the wonderful weight of him.

Then he lay next to her, holding her as if he thought she might break. If she thought about tomorrow, she knew she might.

Instead, she didn't think. Not about Will. Not about Zack. She only felt, losing herself in the heat of this incredible man, as the night slipped away like a thief.

Chapter Fourteen

Samantha wasn't sure at first what had awakened her.
She dragged herself up from an exhausted, contented
sleep to find that she was curled in Will's strong
arms, warm and secure. She smiled, warmed by the
memory of their lovemaking, and closed her eyes as
she snuggled against him.

But her thoughts wouldn't let her fall back to
sleep. She opened her eyes, not sure at first what it
was that was bothering her.

It was the case.

She eased out of Will's arms, pulled on her dry
clothing and padded across the floor into the adjoining room, not wanting to disturb him. Moonlight
streamed through the window. She moved to it, trying to fit the pieces together, something bothering
her, something she couldn't put her finger on.

Outside the window, waves beat the shore, the
moonlight silver on the water.

Five pieces of a game. Cassie had one, Eric, Bradley "Buzz" Guess and Mercedes had all received
one of the CDs in the mail. Now Cassie had hers and
Mercedes's. How did Cassie intend to get the others?

Sam's heart suddenly leapt into her throat. She looked around hurriedly for the phone and realized there wasn't one in the cottage. Her cell phone. It had been in the pickup—not in her purse. She found the keys to the truck where Will had left them on the table and quietly let herself out of the cottage.

Inside the cab of the pickup, she dialed Charley's number. It rang several times before he picked up. A cop was used to getting calls in the middle of the night.

"Charley, it's me, Sam," she said quickly.

"Where the hell are you?" he demanded. "I heard what happened on the ferry. Dammit, Sam—"

"Cassie tried to kill me and I'm afraid she will do anything to get the other pieces of the game—including kill Lucas's partner Bradley Guess and the half-brother, Eric Ross."

"Too late, sweetheart," Charley said quietly. "Bradley Guess was found dead a few hours ago. His piece of the game is missing. And your twenty-four hours are up."

She closed her eyes and squeezed the phone receiver.

"The chief could pull my badge if he finds out I let you—"

"Charley, I don't think it's a game. I think there is something hidden in the game."

"Like what?" he asked. She could tell she had his attention.

"I don't know yet." She thought of what Bebe had said about a way to break into any computer in the world.

"As of this moment, you're off this case," Charley said. "Don't make me pull rank on you. I'd hate to see your butt behind bars, cuz. Worse, mine."

"What about Zack?"

"You leave Zack and Cassie to me," he said confidentially. "There are cops working on this case as we speak. You've repaid any debts you thought you owed Lucas and Zack. You done good. But now it's out of your hands."

She knew he meant it. She was surprised he hadn't demanded she quit when Lucas was found murdered.

"Then I'd better tell you something," she said. "I think I know where the fifth piece of the game is."

"Oh yeah?"

She realized that's what had awakened her. The notes from a song, the same one she'd heard leaking out of Zack's CD player for miles. "I think Zack has it." She explained her theory. "He was so protective of his stuff. It just threw me when I didn't find the CD in his backpack. I should have thought to look in the player."

"You and me both," Charley said. "Where are you, anyway?"

"In some beach cottage with Will," she said almost shyly.

"Good," Charley said with a chuckle. "Stay there. By the way, I think Will is a keeper."

"Me, too." She didn't tell him that Will knew the kind of woman he wanted for his bride—and she wasn't it. "Good night."

"Good night, cuz."

She switched off the cell phone and sat in the darkness of the cab, listening to the waves crashing on the shore and the painful pounding of her heart.

She'd lost Zack. And it was just a matter of time before Will went back to his old life. Worse, she hadn't been able to solve the case and save Zack. Or find Lucas's game.

The cell phone rang, making her jump. She picked it up, thinking it must be Charley calling her back. She'd had enough bad news for one night.

"Sam!" Zack cried. "You have to help—"

Panic seized her heart at the fear in his voice.

Another voice came on the line. "Sam?"

Her heart stuck in her throat, the air around leaden, unbreathable. "Lucas?" she whispered, knowing even as she said his name that it wasn't him. Lucas was dead.

"Do as I tell you," Lucas's voice instructed. "If you don't—" His voice broke off. She could hear Zack in the background crying softly. "You must come alone." She glanced toward the cottage where Will was still sleeping. Leave Will? Her heart felt torn. But nor could she endanger him any more than she already had.

"If you don't, she will kill him," Lucas was saying.

She tried to interrupt but the Lucas voice continued as if he hadn't heard her. Of course he hadn't heard her.

"Listen," he said. "And do exactly as I say."

She listened, understanding only one thing. She'd failed Zack. Now he was in trouble and she had to try to help him. No matter what Charley said.

WILL WOKE TO THE SOUND of a boat. It grew nearer, the soft *putt-putt* of a large motor. He reached across the bed, realizing groggily that the warmth had gone out of the night. Samantha was no longer beside him. The bed was empty!

He sat up with a start. Moonlight splattered across the bare floor, silver shards of light. He jumped up and rushed barefoot and naked into the adjoining room of the cottage, suddenly afraid.

"Samantha?" he called softly.

No answer.

She wasn't in the bathroom or the small kitchen. He glanced toward the front window, not surprised to see the boat he'd heard. It was large—a speedboat dark against the night. He caught his breath. A figure stood silhouetted against the moonlit water. Samantha! She seemed to be waiting on the dock for the approaching boat.

He rushed back into the bedroom and pulled on his still damp jeans and boots. He could hear the boat motor shift into an idle. He ran out of the cottage calling her name. She looked back for an instant, then a hand grabbed her from the boat and pulled her inside. The boat reversed in a growl of engine and a splash of waves.

He reached the dock and almost leaped into the water just as he had from the ferry. But the boat was now too far away. It would have been futile.

The driver slammed the speedboat into gear, and in a thunder of power roared off across the moonlit waves.

Will swore and looked around, spotting a small fishing boat with a 40-horsepower outboard on it at a neighboring dock. The motor started on the second pull, and he aimed the bow of the boat after the disappearing speedboat. The other boat was larger and faster, but he could make out its running lights in the distance. With a little luck—

The wind and waves lashed out at him instantly, sending a shower of spray over the top of the boat and soaking him as he gunned the motor, making him wish he'd grabbed more clothing. He found a slicker in the bottom of the boat, and, although wet, the coat at least provided some protection from the wind.

The small fishing boat skipped along on top of the chop as he followed the retreating speedboat. Why would Samantha leave his bed? She was too smart to go off alone in the dark with some stranger in a boat. What had happened? What would make her do something so dangerous?

Zack. He'd be the only reason. Dear God.

The dark water of the bay moved restlessly. Out here, the wind ripped at the tops of the waves, sending a shower of icy water into the air. Cold and numb, Will kept the bow plowing after the speedboat.

He could barely make out the lights in the distance when he saw that the boat had turned inward and was now headed for shore along a rocky outcropping in what looked like an old industrial area.

He slowed the fishing boat, letting it wallow in the waves as he watched the driver get out of the boat, pulling Samantha with him. The driver hadn't expected to be followed. He didn't even give a backward glance as he dragged Samantha toward what looked like an abandoned building. Will eased the fishing boat toward the shore.

"WHERE ARE YOU taking me?" Samantha demanded, balking at the sight of the deserted building in front of her. Something held her back, a fear that Ralph had tricked her. She wished for Will—and quickly took the wish back. It helped knowing he was back at the cottage, safe. Why in God's name would Zack be here?

The structure had been built to resemble a lighthouse and according to the sign it had once been the Lighthouse Restaurant. A condemned warrant had been stapled over some of the letters of the wooden sign.

"Zack is in there?"

"Waiting for you," Ralph said, grabbing hold of her arm.

She studied the man for a moment, then the building. They both gave her a chill. Ralph was large, and more muscle than brain. That reassured her some; she knew this wasn't his doing. Someone else was calling the shots. Cassie? Belatedly she thought of another blond. Bebe. And Eric. What was it about them that bothered her other than the fact that Eric was a liar? And Bebe was a ditz? Maybe too *much* of a ditz?

Shaking Ralph's hand from her arm, she moved toward the dark shadow of the dilapidated building, a thousand questions whirling like fog in her head. Finally she would know who wanted the game bad enough to kill.

It was dark as she stepped inside the building. Cold and wetness permeated the walls, along with the smell of dead, rotting things. She moved slowly, aware of the man behind her, afraid of the isolation of the place he'd brought her. More afraid of what she'd find once she got deep inside.

"Nice that you could join us—" the woman's voice came from the darkness. "Ralph, wait outside."

Sam squinted, not surprised to see a head of blond hair in the darkness. Cassie. Hadn't she known Cassie was neck deep in all this?

Her eyes adjusted slowly. Only a single dim light shone at the back of the building. It cast odd shadows through the empty shell of the lower floor.

Cassie was sitting on a wooden crate. She didn't appear to be armed. Nor did she move as Sam stepped deeper into the mammoth room. Odd.

"Where is Zack?" Sam demanded as she approached her.

Cassie still didn't move. Nor did she answer. Sam felt cold creep up her spine. As she neared, she saw that Cassie's eyes were open, large and full of fear—and drugs.

"Don't worry, Zack's here."

Sam jumped at the sound of the voice behind her. It was the same female voice she'd heard when she'd entered the building—one she'd mistaken for Cassie's in the hollowed-out, abandoned restaurant.

She spun around. Sam's heart stuck in her throat. For one startled moment she thought there were two Cassies, as a blond woman with a gun emerged from the shadows.

Mercedes smiled. The color and cut of her blond wig were identical to Cassie's. She shoved Zack out of the shadows. The boy stumbled and almost fell, then saw Sam and ran to her. He had a thick piece of tape over his mouth and his hands were bound in front of him.

Sam caught him and hurriedly freed his hands, then eased the tape from his mouth. She pulled the boy into her arms. He hugged her tightly, his heart thumping like a sparrow's. Small almost inaudible sobs tore from his lips.

"Cassie needs a doctor," she said, trying to keep the panic out of her voice as she faced Mercedes. "You've given her too much of whatever it was you used on her."

Mercedes laughed and pulled off the blond wig, exposing the brilliant red of her dyed hair. "Nice try. But it's too late for you to worry about Cassie. Or me." She seemed to notice Samantha searching the corners of darkness in the building. "If you're looking for Lucas, I hate to be the one to tell you, but he's been swimming with the fishes since Friday."

She hadn't been looking for Lucas. But she had been looking for a man—certain Mercedes had one. Certain he would be the man who'd helped Mercedes put her in a bag and carry her to a waiting van.

While the redhead kept the small-caliber gun trained on Sam, she pulled a small recorder from her pocket and depressed a button. Lucas's voice filled the empty building.

"Stop it," Sam snapped, although Zack didn't seem to react.

Mercedes clicked it off, throwing the large empty

building into cold silence again. "Modern technology, Samantha. I would think in your profession you'd be familiar with it. Lucas used his own voice in a lot of his first computer games. With just a little editing..." She smiled. "You don't look well. Don't tell me you still care," Mercedes said tauntingly. "Surely after everything he did to you, you aren't still in love with him?"

Until Will, Sam had wondered if she'd even known what love was or had merely been in love with the idea of a husband and marriage and children. "Why are you doing this?" she asked, hugging Zack to her.

Mercedes shot her a look. "You have to be kidding. Money and power. Is there anything else?" she asked with a laugh.

Apparently not. But at least Mercedes had answered one question. This wasn't about a computer game. Not even a bestselling one. "There is just one thing I don't understand, why give me your piece of the game?"

"To keep you from suspecting me. Except, I hate to bust your bubble, but it wasn't the real CD. Worked though, didn't it?" Mercedes asked with a satisfied smile. "I should have been an actress."

"You must have fooled Lucas," she said. "At least for a while."

"Shut up," Mercedes snarled. "At least he married me."

Sam took the hit, bull's-eye. "Was anything you told me about Lucas true?"

"Everything I told you was true. Except that I

didn't want the game.'' She smiled. ''I lied about
that. So sue me.''

Sam wished she had her purse and the .357 inside
it, but Mercedes had that. She stuffed her hands into
her pockets, her hand closed around the cell phone.
She hit redial.

''What good will your piece do, Mercedes, without the others?'' Sam had a bad feeling that Eric no
longer had his piece of the game any more than Buzz
did. ''Or did you kill Eric the way you did Buzz?''
Answer the phone, Charley. Hear what's going on.

''Eric was much more reasonable than Buzz,'' the
redhead said with a smile. ''He understands the value
of money.''

''What about Bebe?'' Sam asked.

''Bebe?'' Mercedes looked confused. She didn't
know about Bebe?

Sam felt her heart kick up a beat. ''You know,
Mercedes, you could have picked a little nicer place.
An abandoned Lighthouse Restaurant? This really
isn't your style. Where the hell are we anyway?
Down island?''

Mercedes frowned, holding perfectly still, then her
eyes widened. ''Ralph! You searched her before you
brought her in, right?''

Ralph stuck his head in the door, looking confused. ''Her pockets weren't big enough for a gun.''

Mercedes swore and aimed her weapon at Sam's
head. ''Take your hands out of your pockets
slowly.''

Sam had no choice. She removed her hands from

her pockets. "Hey, settle down. I was just cold." She pretended to shiver.

Mercedes swore again. "Ralph! Check her pockets."

Time was up. If Charley hadn't gotten the message—

"Just a cell phone," Ralph said, pulling the compact phone out of her pocket.

"Just a cell phone," Mercedes mimicked before she grabbed the phone and listened for a moment, then punched it off. "You'd better hope that was one wasted call," she said to Sam, her gaze hard as her heart and twice as cold. "Get out of here Ralph before I shoot you."

Sam held her breath as Mercedes hit redial. What would Mercedes do if she heard Charley answer the phone? But he didn't answer. The line seemed to ring and ring. He wasn't home. No doubt he hadn't been home when Sam had tried to call either.

Defeated, she watched Mercedes smile, turn off the phone and hurl it into a dark corner of the building. Something scampered in the phone's wake.

"Nice try, P.I.," Mercedes said in a bad imitation of Bogart, "but I really don't need you anymore. I got the pieces of the game on my own." She waved the gun at Samantha. "Get out of the way, kid."

WILL PULLED THE FISHING BOAT up onto the beach, then stole through the darkness to the large lighthouse building at the end of a long spit of land. It stood in an older industrial area, remote and decaying. He moved through the shadows of rotting buildings until he could see Ralph standing guard outside. A light flickered through the cracks in the walls. An SUV was parked outside, empty.

He moved closer, keeping an eye out for anything he could use as a weapon. He knew Samantha didn't have her gun. It had been in her purse, the purse that Cassie had taken from her on the ferry. But if he knew Sam, she was anything but defenseless. He hoped.

He picked up a rock and a piece of wood the size of a club, then got as close to the lighthouse as he could before heaving the rock into the darkness off to his right.

Ralph jerked around, fumbling to pull a pistol from his jacket. Will was on him quickly, hoping he could keep Ralph from warning whoever was inside the building of his presence.

The wood cracked, sounding loud as it hit Ralph's thick skull. The man barely flinched. For a moment, Will thought he was going to have to hit the guy again. But Ralph's knees buckled, and he dropped like a demolished building.

Will nudged him with a boot toe, but Ralph seemed to be out cold. At least for a while. Hurriedly, Will moved along the side of the building, avoiding gaps in the lumber where light leaked through, just in case someone was watching from inside. He could hear voices but they were too faint for him to make out who was talking.

He reached the door. It stood ajar. He stopped to peer through the opening. He could see Samantha and Zack, could hear Zack crying, "No! No!"

He heard another voice. Someone was holding a gun on Samantha and Zack.

''No! Don't hurt her!'' Zack cried.

Will grabbed the edge of the door, and would have gone busting in like the cavalry with only a piece of rotting wood and no plan— But he didn't get the chance. The barrel of a gun poked into his back and a low voice warned him not to make a move.

Chapter Fifteen

"Well, look who's here," Mercedes said almost cheerfully as she looked past Samantha and Zack to the doorway.

Her sudden mood swing scared Sam almost as much as the gun in the woman's manicured hand. She turned and her heart stopped at the sight of Will standing in the doorway. No! her mind screamed.

He smiled at her, a smile that could have melted frozen pizza. Behind him Bobby Walker looked less friendly out of his tennis attire. And that definitely wasn't a racket he clutched in his hand. Sam felt her heart sink.

"Will doesn't have anything to do with this," she said, turning to Mercedes, who was obviously running this show.

"He does now," Mercedes said, motioning for Will to move closer to Sam and Zack. Now she had them in her sights and Bobby was behind them, armed with yet another weapon.

Sam realized that if she hadn't been so convinced Cassie was behind all of this, she'd have seen it sooner. Mercedes and Bobby. She'd broken all her rules on this case, starting with the worst of all, getting too personally involved.

She'd screwed up and now they were in terrible trouble. What chance did they have against Mercedes and Bobby with both of them armed? And where was Ralph?

"Let me guess," Sam said, stalling for time as she tried to come up with a plan. "You married Lucas because you'd heard about what he was working on. I'll bet it was your idea to bring in the 'investor.' Lucas must have gotten wise to you, though, and divorced you. But why send you a piece of the game then?"

Mercedes smiled. "Actually, I let Lucas think it was his idea, the marriage, the investor and the divorce. We just weren't compatible, you know, but he owed me. I'd gotten him an investor so he didn't have to live on the street until he finished the damn *game*."

"But, of course, it isn't just a game," Sam said.

Mercedes narrowed her gaze. "You are so right, gumshoe. It's far from a game."

"The problem is," Sam said, hoping she was right about this, "you don't have all five pieces." Sam could see Zack's backpack lying near Mercedes's feet but Zack still had the CD player, the headphones around his neck.

"The last piece will turn up," Mercedes said confidently. "I had hoped you'd find it for me. But whoever has it will eventually come for the kid. I'll be waiting."

Sam felt her heart drop. Mercedes's plan actually could work. It was just a matter of time before the redhead had all the pieces. Sam wondered, though, if Bobby had heard his girlfriend's slip? "Did you hear that, Bobby? She said, 'I'll be waiting.' How long do you think you'll last once she doesn't need you anymore?"

"Save it," Mercedes snapped. "Bobby loves me. He knows I wouldn't harm a hair on his head." She shot a look at Bobby. "Don't listen to her, lover."

"What about Zack?" Will asked.

Mercedes sent the boy a withering look. "Children have accidents all the time. It really is quite horrid. I'm amazed so many live through childhood."

Sam's blood turned to ice.

"Now, just a minute," Bobby cried. "You said no one would get hurt. If you hadn't had to kill Lucas then that stupid wrestler—"

"Shut up, Bobby," Mercedes snapped.

"Oh, the head count is more than that," Sam said, wondering if maybe Bobby Walker was starting to realize what kind of woman he'd hooked up with. "She's killed Bradley Guess as well."

"Mercedes!" Bobby cried, looking at her with horror. "You said there wouldn't be any more."

"Plans change, you sniveling fool," Mercedes barked. "Now shut up. You're giving me a headache."

"But you said no one was going to get hurt," Bobby persisted.

"That makes you an accomplice to murder," Will pointed out to Bobby.

"Enough," Mercedes yelled and fired a shot up into the ceiling. The report wasn't loud because of the silencer on the gun but dust and dirt showered down, stilling everyone in the room.

Sam heard Cassie groan.

''Get the damned boy out of the way and let me finish this,'' Mercedes ordered Bobby.

Zack clung to Sam's legs, refusing to let go. For a moment, Sam thought Bobby would refuse. He had a gun. Maybe he'd stop all of this right now by turning it on Mercedes.

No such luck. He hesitated, but then came toward Sam and Zack. Sam tried to shield the boy from him but Bobby tore Zack from her, shoving her back as he dragged the boy over to Mercedes. Mercedes's weapon never wavered on Sam and Will.

''Just do it and get it over with!'' Bobby said impatiently and looked at his watch. He probably had a tennis game first thing in the morning.

''No!'' Zack cried. ''I have the other piece of the game!''

''Zack, don't—'' But Sam's words were lost in Zack's.

''Don't hurt her or Will,'' the boy said as he slid the earphones from around his neck and opened the CD player.

Sam shook her head at the boy. ''I know you want to help, but we all know the game isn't in your CD,'' she tried to bluff.

''I don't want them to hurt you,'' he said sounding years older than he was. He carefully lifted the disk from the player.

Even from this distance, Sam could see the blood-red letters: Catastrophe. The CD was exactly where she knew it would be. And now Mercedes had all of the pieces—and no reason to leave any of them alive.

"My dad told me not to give it to anyone," Zack said, looking at Sam.

Her heart fractured like thin glass at the thought of the boy keeping his father's secret all this time. "You did great, Zack," she said, her voice breaking. "Your dad would have been proud of you."

"Give me that!" Mercedes snapped, almost salivating as she took the disk from him.

Sam glanced at Will. His eyes glittered with emotion and something more. He flicked his gaze toward a dark wall off to her left. She moved her head slowly to look in the direction he indicated. A rusty old shovel stood against the wall. A weapon.

"Get my computer out of the car," Mercedes ordered Bobby. She reached for her car keys and stopped, her face suddenly distorted in rage. "You little bugger!" she spat at Zack. "Give me my keys."

Zack hesitated, but only for a moment before he dug her car keys from his pocket and handed them to her.

"You see what I mean about this kid?" she demanded of Sam.

Sam had hoped Bobby would leave and help the odds. But the moment Bobby left, Mercedes grabbed Zack and held the gun to his back as they waited for her boyfriend to return with the laptop.

Bobby dragged up some boards and put the computer on it. Mercedes popped in the first disk and added Zack's disk to the others in a neat little pile.

She looked very pleased with herself. She motioned with the gun for Zack to come closer.

"I used to watch you sitting on your father's lap while he worked," Mercedes said. "You know how to put these together, don't you?"

Realization dawned. No wonder Mercedes had wanted Zack—as well as the pieces of the game.

With a defeated look, Zack moved to the computer.

"Aren't you forgetting something?" Bobby asked and motioned toward Sam and Will.

Mercedes studied them for a moment.

"If you hurt them I won't show you how the pieces go together," Zack said in that older voice that made Sam want to cry. The boy had been through so much.

Mercedes motioned for Bobby to shut up. "Sure, kid. Just show me."

Zack looked over at Sam, waiting for her to tell him what to do.

She nodded. "It's okay, Zack." At best, it would buy them a little time. Otherwise, Mercedes would figure the pieces out for herself. There wasn't any doubt that once she knew how they went together, however, that she'd kill them all.

"You do it like this," Zack said, and got down on his knees. Familiar music filled the room as bright-colored graphics filled the screen.

Sam watched as he adeptly moved the mouse and things began to happen on the screen. New music soared. Images flashed.

Sam watched in awe, having no idea how high-tech computer games had become. Landscapes flew by, figures leaped from spots on the wall, rock music boomed and Zack moved through the game like a race car driver, weaving in and out, dodging evil forces, his movements quick, his gaze intent, his shoulders taut as he worked the mouse.

It dawned on Sam that the computer had been the one constant in Zack's life. This was something he'd been doing since he was old enough to sit on his father's lap while he worked.

She waited, wondering what was really inside the game, what was worth killing so many people for, fearing she already knew.

Zack popped another disk into the CD-ROM and Bobby and Mercedes moved closer to watch. Sam inched toward the shovel. If she could reach it, she would be within striking distance of Bobby. All she knew for sure was that she had to get Zack and Will out of this or die trying.

WILL HELD his breath as Sam moved toward the shovel. True to form, he improvised a plan. It was risky. But he knew with certainty that Mercedes planned to kill them.

He wasn't concerned for his own welfare, but he couldn't let anything happen to Sam. Or Zack. If he could help it.

Zack popped in another disk. More music. More wild graphics. Mercedes's gaze seemed glued to the screen as if hypnotized by what she saw there. But the barrel of her pistol was still pointed in his direction and Sam's. Bobby's weapon was aimed downward, his attention completely on the computer screen.

Will moved the moment Samantha's hand closed over the shovel handle. She grabbed the shovel and swung. Will dove at the same time for Zack. The air filled with the sound of the metal of the shovel clanging off the gun in Bobby's hand and the investor's howl of pain. Mercedes added to the melee as Will slammed her out of his way to get to Zack.

Out of the corner of Will's eye, he saw Samantha give Bobby one of her chops and kicks. The investor went down face-first in the dirt.

Will came up with Zack in his arms.

But Mercedes was very fast on her feet. Worse, she hadn't dropped her gun in the fall. She came at him, all wild-eyed, her red hair like a wound. He turned, trying to shelter Zack, as she swung wildly at them. The gun butt connected with Will's skull. He felt Zack being jerked from his arms just before the lights blinked out.

"Stupid, stupid, stupid," Mercedes spat as she grabbed Zack around the neck and dragged him at gunpoint back to the computer.

SAM HAD no choice but to back off. She had tried to get to Mercedes before the redhead could reach Will, but hadn't been able to. Now he lay sprawled on the ground, a cut over his right temple, the wound bleeding into the dirt. She wanted desperately to go to him, but she held her ground, seeing murder in Mercedes's eyes. *Oh, Will, why didn't I just leave you alone? If you hadn't followed me out to the library terrace that night and if I hadn't kissed you—*

"Finish it," the redhead ordered Zack.

Sam watched as he put in disk after disk, until

finally he reached for disk five. Time was running out, and she had no plan. Fear welled inside her— cold and dark and unrelenting fear. She couldn't save Zack any more than she had saved Will.

Music soared and the laptop's screen seemed to vibrate with color and motion. "I'll be damned," Mercedes breathed.

And Sam knew it was over.

"The bastard was telling the truth," Mercedes said.

Sam could see the screen. "Let me guess. Lucas wrote some software that would allow him to break into any computer in the world without detection." The magnitude of that didn't escape her. No computer would be safe, from banks to governments to Fort Knox.

"And he hid it in one of his stupid computer games," Mercedes said. "Pure genius."

Sam had a sudden thought. "What about the men he owes money to? Won't they be looking for this?"

Mercedes gave her a smug smile. "Come on, Sam, there were no guys. Other than Al and Ralph. I paid off all Lucas's debts but made him think Al and Ralph were goons hired to collect. I have a little genius in me as well."

So this was the end of the line. No chance of rescue. And on top of that, Bobby was starting to groan as if he was waking up.

Sam understood now why Lucas had divided the game into five pieces. He'd hoped to outsmart the goons after him and eventually pick up the pieces. He didn't have any idea the kind of people after him.

"I don't understand why you didn't just go in with

Lucas,'' Sam said. "Then no one would have had to die. Or were you just too greedy to share even that much money and power?"

Mercedes made a disgusted sound. "I would have gone into business with him. But Lucas—" she spat out the word with distaste "—sold himself to Cassie for the price of a dinky, worthless computer business. But when he finally has the ability to really make some money, what does he do? He gets a conscience and starts talking about what sort of legacy he'd be leaving his son if he didn't do the *right* thing."

Sam stared at her. "Lucas talked to you about the software?"

"Only on theoretical terms. Of course, I agreed with him that he should *give* it to some government agency so it didn't fall into the wrong hands—should he ever design something so inherently harmful to mankind." Mercedes made a disgusted face. "So the fool sent me one of the pieces of the game and he called it Catastrophe. Lucas's little attempt at humor."

Sam realized Bebe had been right, but no one had believed the ditzy blonde.

"Funny, but it only turned out to be a catastrophe for him—and, of course, you," Mercedes said. "If only he could see the *legacy* he left his son now." She pushed Zack away from the computer. He stumbled over to Sam and she pulled him into her arms.

"You promised," the boy cried as Mercedes raised her gun to fire.

In that split second, Sam thought she heard a sound outside the building. A shuffle of feet. But realized belatedly it was probably just Ralph.

Mercedes aimed at the boy before Sam could get between him and the gun. She pulled the trigger.

Cassie came out of nowhere. Drugged and stumbling, she managed to throw herself in front of Zack, taking the bullet meant for her son.

Mercedes started to fire again. But as Sam scrambled to get Zack out of her line of fire, she heard Will moan. Then suddenly he kicked Mercedes's legs out from under her. She went down hard. The wild shot brought down more dust and dirt.

Then Will was standing and holding Mercedes and Bobby at gunpoint with the redhead's weapon, looking like only determination was keeping him on his feet.

Before Sam and Zack could rush to him, Charley was there and cops were swarming all over. Charley grabbed Mercedes, and snapped on the cuffs as Bebe began to read the redhead her rights.

Bebe. An undercover cop. Just as Sam had suspected. The blonde smiled over at her as she snapped cuffs on Bobby. "You just invested in a lot of years in prison," she said as she jerked him to his feet and began to read him his rights.

In the distance, Sam could hear sirens screaming their way toward them. She stumbled with Zack over to Will. His head was bleeding where Mercedes had hit him.

"Will. You're hurt," Sam cried.

"An ambulance is on its way," Charley said. "You're all right? And Zack?"

She nodded.

"Then get Zack out of here," her cousin ordered,

"and we'll discuss just what you were doing here later."

She clutched Zack and Will to her as they stumbled outside to the sound of the ambulance's siren. She refused to leave Will's side so she and Zack were allowed to ride in the ambulance to the hospital with him.

It wasn't until later, after he'd been admitted for a possible concussion, that Sam broke down, her relief flowing out as tears as she hugged Zack and cried.

"Is he going to be okay?" Zack asked in a small scared voice.

"Yeah, he has to be, huh," she said as she stared down at Will's sleeping form. The first light of day bled through the hospital room window. "He has to be okay."

Chapter Sixteen

"Zack?" Cassie whispered when she opened her eyes.

Sam moved closer to the hospital bed. The monitors beeped and whirred. Cassie lay white against the sheets. "Zack's fine."

Cassie smiled and closed her eyes, the worry lines smoothing in her face. "Lucas did love him, you know." She opened her eyes and seemed to fight for each breath. "Zack just needed a mother and a father. I should never have left him." Regret burned in her eyes. It was too late to change things now, but Sam suspected Cassie knew that.

"I want to adopt Zack."

Cassie smiled. "I knew you would," she whispered. "But there is something you must know. Zack—" She sucked in a ragged breath.

"Don't try to talk."

"No, I have to tell you about Zack's father," Cassie managed to get out. "It's Charley."

At first Sam thought she'd misunderstood. They'd all been going to college at the same time but... Cassie and Charley? She searched Cassie's face and saw the truth. She thought of Zack's dark hair and eyes. Why hadn't Sam seen the resemblance? It was so obvious now that she thought about it. Zack even made some of the same facial expressions as Charley.

"It's up to you whether you tell him," Cassie said, her voice so low that Sam had to lean down to hear her. "Your decision." Cassie took another gasp of air, tried to say something, but stopped herself. Instead, she motioned to the table beside the hospital bed.

Sam pulled open the drawer and saw a piece of white paper. At Cassie's insistence, she drew it out. Cassie had gotten the nurse to draw up a paper and had paved the way for Sam to adopt Zack. The paper had been signed and witnessed.

Sam's eyes blurred with tears. She looked at the woman lying in the bed and reached for her hand. "Thank you."

Cassie shook her head slowly. "I just needed to know—" she sucked in another breath, her face drawn with pain "—Zack is going to be all right now."

The monitor beside Cassie's bed went off, a shrill frightening sound. Several nurses raced into the room and ordered Sam out.

"I promise I'll take care of him," Sam called to Cassie as she was pushed back. A crash cart was rushed into the room. She held the precious paper to her as she stumbled out into the hall.

She stayed there, captured by the frantic sounds inside the room she'd just left until the doctor came out to tell her that Cassie was gone.

Then she stood in the hallway and cried, cried for Cassie and Lucas and Zack and Charley and Katie, and for herself and Will. She didn't cry long. Then, wiping her eyes, she went to find her cousin.

WILL LOOKED UP FROM his hospital bed to see Charley Murphy framed in the doorway.

"Mind if I come in?"

"Not at all, I could use the company," he said, and smiled. He hadn't seen Charley since last night and he hadn't been in any shape then to thank him. "Thanks for your help."

Charley shrugged. "Part of the job. I'm just glad I got Sam's call and could get there in time. You were the real heroes, though."

"Yeah, right," he said. "How is Cassie?"

Charley shook his head. "I'm grateful for what you did, helping Sam. And Zack."

Will nodded. "Something tells me you didn't just come by to build up my self-esteem."

Charley shook his head. "I need to know how you feel about my cousin."

"Yeah, I thought that might be it." Will took a deep breath. "Twenty-five words or less? I'm crazy about her. I can't imagine living a day without her. But I also can't imagine living a day with her working as a private investigator. It scares the hell out of me. I've always thought of myself as a pretty progressive kind of guy. But I'm not sure I can be married to a woman who risks her life like that."

"That's kind of what I thought," Charley said.

Samantha stuck her head in the door then, almost

as if on cue. "Hi," she said, and smiled at him. "How are you feeling?"

He nodded. He'd forgotten just how beautiful she was. The bright blue morning and the sunshine streaming in the window gave her a glow that pretty near made him take back everything he'd just told Charley and turn those words into a proposal of marriage. Pretty near.

But he could also see that she'd been crying. "What is it?" he asked.

"Cassie. She just passed away," Sam said.

He could see her fighting more tears.

"Mind if I steal Charley for a moment?" she asked, her voice hoarse with emotion.

He noticed tension then in her eyes, and feared why she'd come to talk to her cousin. He thought of Zack. The boy had lost both his mother and the only father he'd known.

A nurse stuck her head in the doorway. "Good news! The doctor said you can leave this morning," she said cheerfully. "By the way," she said holding up his chart, "happy birthday."

"Thanks." His thirty-sixth birthday. And he could go home. It seemed like eons since the day he'd driven to Wolf Point to bid a job and seen Samantha sitting in the sun in her Firebird. Or one of her cousins' Firebird. He never had gotten around to asking her just whose car it was. Not that it mattered now.

He realized he should call his sister. Katherine was probably worried about him. Yeah, right.

"Where have you been?" she demanded the moment she heard his voice on the phone. "You've heard what happened? The commissioner has been arrested. Someone captured him on film exchanging construction bills for cash at *my* party! In *my* library!''

''Really?'' He smiled, remembering the beautiful young woman he'd followed to the library terrace with two glasses of cold champagne. ''Imagine that.''

''Where are you? It almost sounds like you're in a hospital,'' Katherine said, obviously overhearing a page for one of the doctors on call. ''Will? Will, what's happened?''

He didn't know where to start. But as was his nature, he started from the beginning.

When he finished, Katherine said, ''You risked your life for this woman and child?''

He guessed he had. He realized he'd do it again.

''That is so unlike you,'' his sister was saying. ''Just taking off like that. Tell me more about this woman. Murphy? Samantha Murphy, right?''

This time when he finished, his sister said, ''Oh, Will,'' and he realized she was crying. ''Jennifer Finley will be so disappointed.''

SAMANTHA AND CHARLEY WALKED down the hall to one of the hospital atriums. They had the space to themselves and stood for a moment, neither talking.

''Cassie is gone,'' she said after a moment.

He said nothing, just stared at the floor. ''I know. I'm sorry.''

''She signed a paper making me Zack's legal guardian and asking that I be allowed to adopt him.'' Her voice broke with emotion.

He looked up quickly. ''Is that what you want?''

"More than anything." She hesitated. "Before she died, she told me who Zack's father is."

Charley's gaze met hers and held it, gentle and yet solid as a rock. That was Charley. She felt her heart begin to pound and tears welled again in her eyes. "How long have you known?"

He shook his head. "Not until the day that Cassie came by the house with the court order to pick Zack up. I guess something just clicked. I remembered that one night we'd spent together and suddenly I looked at Zack as she left with him—and realized he was mine. Do you know he's going to have my big feet? Poor kid," he added with a laugh.

"You and Cassie," she said, shaking her head.

"It was only one night. I had no idea she had conceived, since we used protection. But nothing is failsafe, huh?"

"She didn't realize she was pregnant with your baby until after you met Katie and fell in love with her," Sam said.

"She still should have told me," he said, then shook his head, obviously thinking how that would have changed all of their lives.

"What about Katie?"

Charley smiled. "I told her. She says she's fine with whatever I decide to do."

Sam held her breath. "What are you going to do?"

"Tell Zack the truth. Someday. When he's older. Right now he's confused enough. He's just lost the only father he's ever known. For now, Lucas was Zack's father. Let's leave it at that."

"What are you saying?" she asked, her heart in her throat.

"That it's time for you to tell Will what happened five years ago," Charley said. "He loves you and I know you love him. Clean the slate. Tell him everything. Then decide what it is you want and go for it."

"I already know what I want." She held his gaze. "I want Will. And Zack."

Charley nodded. "It's obvious that Zack loves you and Will, and that the two of you feel the same way about him." He stopped as if overcome with emotion. "I couldn't bear not to see Zack grow up now that I know about him. But I will be able to, as your son, Sam. And my nephew."

She threw her arms around her cousin's neck.

He held her for a long moment. "So what are you waiting for?"

"Courage," she whispered.

"Cousin," he said, holding her at arm's length. "You have more courage than any woman I've ever known. And more love to give. You're going to make Zack a great mother."

She hugged Charley once more, then headed for Will's room.

WHEN SAMANTHA PUSHED OPEN the door to Will's room, her heart fell at the sight of the stripped bed. She'd missed him! He'd already gone home.

Then she heard him. He was on the phone. She stepped in and saw him sitting in the alcove by the window.

"It has to be a bright-red boy's bike," he was saying. "You have one in stock that size? Great! I'm going to have to get back to you about where to deliver it. No problem." He hung up, smiling.

Seeing the happiness in his face, she started to back out of the room. She didn't want to add any more pain. After all, she'd almost gotten him killed, not to mention everything else she'd put him through the past few days. He must be anxious to get back to his old life. That's where he belonged.

But before she could escape, he seemed to sense her, and turned. "Samantha," he said softly.

"They're letting you leave," she said lamely. "That's good. I guess you're all right?"

He nodded, his gaze intent on her face. "My head's too hard for something like a gun butt to do much damage," he said, motioning to the clean white bandage on his temple. "Just a slight concussion."

She couldn't go through with this. No matter what Charley said. "I need to tell you something."

"I need to tell you something, too," Will said.

Oh boy, here we go.

"You don't have to say anything," she said quickly. "I already know."

"You do?" He sounded surprised.

She nodded, unable to speak for a moment. "I want to tell you about Lucas and me."

He frowned. "Yes?"

"Five years ago, after I found out about Cassie and Lucas, I did something really stupid. I was upset, and I got into my car and I started driving." She stopped for breath. "It was snowing out and the roads were slick and I was crying."

"I know you had a car wreck," he said quietly.

She nodded and took another breath. "But what

you don't know, that no one but Charley knows, is that—'' The tears came in a wave. She choked back a sob.

Will rushed to her and took her in his arms. "It's all right, Sam. Whatever it is, it's all right."

"I was pregnant with Lucas's baby." The words were out. Finally. "I was pregnant and I killed my baby in the wreck."

All the guilt, all the grief, all the pain she'd held inside her for five years came out in a flood.

"Oh, Sam," Will whispered as he hugged her. "Oh, Sam." She cried then for all she'd lost. For the little baby who had ended her dream of motherhood and marriage with Lucas.

Will held her until her tears waned, then got her a cold washcloth and waited while she pressed it to her face.

"I'm glad you told me," he said after a few moments. "I knew something else had happened to you. I thought it was just Lucas."

She shook her head.

"He never knew?"

She shook her head again. "He was already planning to marry Cassie." She straightened her shoulders and looked him in the eye. "There's one more thing."

He braced himself.

"It's Zack. Cassie told me who his father is."

"Charley."

She stared at him. "You already knew?"

"Suspected as much. The resemblance is amazing, added to the fact that you all went to college at the same time." He grinned at her. "Is it my turn?"

"Not just yet," she said, and seemed to fortify herself. "I intend to adopt Zack. Before Cassie died she asked that I be made legal guardian."

He nodded, not surprised.

"Aren't you going to say anything?"

"What about your private investigator work?"

"I have quite a bit of money saved. I can keep the agency open and hire investigators and stay at home and raise Zack."

He studied her. "Is that what you really want?"

She seemed to soften. "It's what I always wanted. I almost had it once, and when I lost it— Well, I told myself I wanted a career, something hard-hitting, even dangerous."

"And now?" he asked, afraid he was either dreaming or delirious.

"I want to make a family for Zack," she said confidently.

He raised a brow. "All by yourself?"

"A lot of single women raise children alone nowadays," she said, lifting her chin.

He had to smile. "Yeah, but Zack needs a father. An in-house father. And I need a bride."

"Will—"

He silenced her with a kiss. "I thought I knew exactly what I was looking for in a bride. When I saw you, I knew you were the one. Then I got to know you." He laughed.

"If this is your idea of sweeping me off my feet, it isn't working," she pointed out.

He cupped her face in his hands. "I kept telling myself that I couldn't live with a P.I. for a wife. But I realized something when I was telling my sister about you. You might not be what I planned in a bride, but you are exactly what I want. I'm wildly, passionately, crazy in love with you.''

''Much better,'' she said, smiling up into his eyes.

''I love you, Samantha Murphy. I want to marry you and adopt Zack and have a dozen more kids. We can live in Butte or Billings or wherever you want. I'll build us a house, large enough for your whole family. If you want to be a private eye or a mortician or a jet pilot, I don't care. Whatever you want, Sam, just say you'll be my bride.''

She smiled, feeling like Cinderella all over again. With tears in her eyes, she leaned up to kiss her prince. ''I love you, too, Will, but are you sure you know what you're getting into?''

''With you I *never* know,'' he said, and laughed as he drew her to him. ''But I wouldn't have it any other way. Let's go get Zack and tell him the news! Oh yeah, and we have to pick up a bright-red bicycle on the way.''

Harlequin invites you to walk down the aisle…

To honor our year long celebration of weddings, we are offering an exciting opportunity for you to own the Harlequin Bride Doll. Handcrafted in fine bisque porcelain, the wedding doll is dressed for her wedding day in a cream satin gown accented by lace trim. She carries an exquisite traditional bridal bouquet and wears a cathedral-length dotted Swiss veil. Embroidered flowers cascade down her lace overskirt to the scalloped hemline; underneath all is a multi-layered crinoline.

Join us in our celebration of weddings by sending away for your own Harlequin Bride Doll. This doll regularly retails for $74.95 U.S./approx. 108.68 CDN. One doll per household. Requests must be received no later than June 30, 2001. Offer good while quantities of gifts last. Please allow 6-8 weeks for delivery. Offer good in the U.S. and Canada only. Become part of this exciting offer!

Simply complete the order form and mail to:
"A Walk Down the Aisle"

IN U.S.A
P.O. Box 9057
3010 Walden Ave.
Buffalo, NY 14240-9057

IN CANADA
P.O. Box 622
Fort Erie, Ontario
L2A 5X3

Enclosed are eight (8) proofs of purchase found on the last page of every specially marked Harlequin series book and $3.75 check or money order (for postage and handling). Please send my Harlequin Bride Doll to:

_____
Name (PLEASE PRINT)

_____
Address   Apt. #

_____
City   State/Prov.   Zip/Postal Code

_____
Account # (if applicable)   **098 KIK DAEW**

Visit us at www.eHarlequin.com

PHWDAPOP

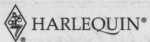
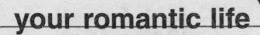